LOCKDOWN FANTASY #1

Compiled & Edited by

D. Kershaw | Maggie Pawsey | S.N. Graves

Also available and coming soon from Black Hare Press

DARK DRABBLES ANTHOLOGIES

WORLDS

ANGELS

MONSTERS

BEYOND

UNRAVEL

APOCALYPSE

LOVE

HATE

OCEANS

ANCIENTS

BHP WRITERS' GROUP SPECIAL EDITIONS

STORMING AREA 51

EERIE CHRISTMAS

BAD ROMANCE

TWENTY TWENTY

OTHER VOLUMES

DEEP SPACE

WHAT IF?

KEY TO THE KINGDOM

DEEP SEA

BEYOND THE REALM

Twitter: @BlackHarePress

Facebook: BlackHarePress

Website: www.BlackHarePress.com

Cover Design	Dawn Burdett	www.dmburdett.com
Formatting	Ben Thomas	www.blackharepress.com
Editing	D. Kershaw	www.blackharepress.com
	Maggie Pawsey	
	S.N. Graves	www.sngraves.com
Read Team	David Green	davidgreenwritercom.wordpress.com
	Jennifer Hatfield	jhatfieldauthor.wixsite.com/website
	Jodi Jensen	jodijensenwrites.wordpress.com
	Lyndsay Ellis-Holloway	authorlyndseyellisholloway.webador.co.uk
	Stacey Jaine McIntosh	www.staceyjainemcintosh.com

TABLE OF CONTENTS

RAVEN

By Rich Rurshell

"What's your name, kid?"

She peered out from behind the dusty wreckage of the old war machine. The piercing green eyes of a large, grey tomcat stared back at her.

"It's safe now. You can come out."

She came out from behind the twisted metal, never taking her eyes from the tomcat.

"I'm DiTillio. I'll introduce you to the family." He jumped up onto what was left of a brick wall.

"I don't have a name," she said.

"Mother Eve will name you soon enough. You won't be the first orphan stray to join the family." DiTillio disappeared over the wall.

On the other side of the wall, she saw the bloody corpses of the hounds that had been hunting her moments before. DiTillio had joined four other cats at the feet of a human woman. The woman's grey, matted hair hung around her shoulders from beneath a brown Fedora hat. She wore a long coat, possibly once beige, but now stained with mud, blood and the dust which blew across the lands from day to day. DiTillio rubbed his head against her faded black cowboy boots, and she dropped some scraps of meat from her pocket to him.

"Who have we here, DiTillio?"

DiTillio beckoned to the little stray. The other cats moved aside, allowing her to approach the old woman. The woman smiled.

"Come, come, little one! We've plenty here to fill your tum!" The woman chuckled and tossed some meat onto the ground.

The stray cat wasted no time snapping up the food. The woman grinned, watching the little kitten eat up the scraps.

"A ravenous little stray I see; Raven, then your name shall be!" She dropped a few more scraps of meat at her feet, and made her way over to a rusty old shopping cart full of sacks and plastic bags. The cats devoured the food before it had barely touched the ground.

"Raven eh? Cute. That's Mother Eve, anyway. You can trust her, she's not like most humans. She lost her family to the gangs and the mutants, so we're her family now." DiTillio looked over to the other cats. "The two tabbies are Coltrane and Davis. They're brothers. We found them about a month ago. Strays, just like you."

The brothers nodded to Raven, then continued playing with an old scrap of leather on the ground.

"The red-hair is Jock. He's pretty old now, but don't let that fool you. He could tear you to ribbons in the shake of a whisker."

"Aye. Nice to meet you, Raven. DiTillio speaks the truth, but you're one of us now, so you're safe." Jock winked.

"And your fellow feline female of darkness here is Weaver."

Weaver looked Raven up and down and turned her back. The black cat left the others and joined Mother Eve at the shopping cart.

"Don't take it personally, kid. Weaver is always like that with new folk."

"Mother Eve killed the hounds?" asked Raven.

"Yes," replied DiTillio. "And their owners."

"Not by herself, mind," said Jock. "It was a team effort."

Raven watched as Mother Eve pushed the cart over to a dead human on the ground and began rifling through the pockets of its garments.

"Why do the humans kill one another?"

"A twisted form of survival, I suppose," answered Jock. "Everything is scarce now. Food, water, weapons, tools. The fewer humans there are, the more stuff there is to go around."

"It's not all of them, though. There are still some good humans alive," said DiTillio. "Most are in hiding. Some managed to stockpile supplies and find a safe haven. Others have to go out and scavenge, just as the gangs do. The gangs are unscrupulous. They'll kill any rivals or innocents they come across to cut down the competition. They often round up stray dogs and train them to hunt. They starve them and beat them, which makes them obedient, but violent. I pity them really, but I have no qualms about Mother Eve blasting them to pieces if they attack. It's them or us."

"We all have a common enemy though," said Jock.

"We do?"

"The mutants."

"The mutants?"

"Aye. The only time you should be

happy to see the gangs is when mutants are around."

"The gangs are heavily armed and see hunting mutants as sport. They are tough to kill, ferocious, and insane. Born corrupted in the contaminated zones, those that don't die from poisoning within the radiation fields, stray out into the safe zones and roam the lands searching for food. They'll eat anything, or anyone." DiTillio looked at Mother Eve for a moment and turned back to Raven. "Mutants got Mother Eve's husband, Shlomo."

"Aye. There was nothing left of the poor bastard," added Jock. "Got him on his own outside the shelter we were living in. We heard his screams, but we were too late. We lost two other cats that day too. Bert and Bluey."

Coltrane and Davis had stopped playing and were listening in silence.

"There were five of them. Four of them were small. Rabbits or hares or something. Hard to tell. Bigger than normal, but we took them out fairly easily. There was a big one with them though. Some sort of deformed stag it was. Took us all the best part of an hour to kill it. Mother Eve put so many holes in that thing, but it just kept coming. Almost used her entire stockpile of ammunition. Only me, DiTillio, Weaver, and Mother Eve survived it."

"That's when we left on our pilgrimage," said DiTillio.

"Your pilgrimage? To where?"

"Home."

"Where is home?"

A shrill whistle interrupted them. Coltrane, Davis, and Jock bounded off towards Mother Eve.

"Time to go, kid. I'll explain on the way."

***

"Hounds!" cried Mother Eve. She stooped down and picked up Raven and tossed her into the cart. She picked up a long, leather sleeve from the cart and dropped to one knee.

Raven watched as Coltrane and Davis darted away towards the barking, and the other cats scattered into hiding places. Two

Dobermanns and a Bullmastiff charged towards them from between two rundown storage containers. Coltrane and Davis split up and ran away from the approaching dogs. The Dobermanns went for Coltrane, the Bullmastiff for Davis. There was a deafening blast from behind Raven and the Bullmastiff tumbled into the dust in a mist of red. Its yelping was promptly cut short with a second blast from Mother Eve's rifle.

Coltrane scrambled up a wire fence with the Dobermanns inches behind him. Weaver and DiTillio reappeared and circled the two dogs jumping up against the fence. Weaver hissed and the two dogs changed their intended target. Weaver and DiTillio bolted away. Again, Mother Eve pulled the trigger of her rifle. A glass door panel behind one of the dogs exploded, and she cursed and reloaded. Raven cowered amongst the foul-smelling sacks within the shopping cart.

Other gunshots echoed down the street as two humans appeared from behind the storage containers.

"Shit." Mother Eve dropped the rifle and reached into the cart. She took out a plastic bag, and then ran for cover behind a burnt-out car wreck, leaving Raven alone in the cart.

Weaver and DiTillio had unsuccessfully tried to separate the Dobermanns, and both had gone for Weaver. She had found her way up to the tattered awning of an empty convenience store, the dogs barking and jumping up at her, jaws snapping.

"Smith! Wesson! Get back over here," shouted one of the humans.

The Dobermanns turned and began to race towards their owners, but suddenly changed course and began barking and charging at the burnt-out car.

"That's it, boys! Go get that old bitch!" The humans fired several shots at the car wreck and advanced.

Jock darted out from his hiding place and pounced onto the face of one of the Dobermanns, biting and clawing at the soft flesh. The dog snarled and shook him off, and Jock sprinted away. The wounded Dobermann gave chase, and the other continued towards Mother Eve.

Davis crossed paths with Jock on his retreat, and for a moment, the pursuing dog faltered. Jock scaled the wire fence and vanished. The Dobermann set off after Davis.

Coltrane tried to attract the attention of the other dog, but Mother Eve was now its target.

"Go get her, Wesson! Good boy!" The two humans broke into a run as their hound tore towards Mother Eve. A short sharp burst of rapid gunfire sent the Dobermann sprawling to the ground. A second killed it.

Mother Eve came out from cover, her sub-machine gun spraying bullets down the street towards her attackers. They both dropped to the ground. Blood poured from the eye socket of one of them as he twitched in the dust. The other returned fire, emptying his pistol. Mother Eve cried out and fell down. As the remaining human reloaded his gun, Mother Eve dragged herself towards the shopping cart. Before the man could fire, Weaver appeared and viciously clawed at his face. He managed to get hold of one of her legs as they scrambled in the dust, and then pinned her to the ground by her neck. He picked up his pistol and brought it to Weaver's head.

His face exploded, and he slumped down on top of Weaver.

Mother Eve rolled over with the rifle to find the other Dobermann, blood gushing from a wound in her thigh. Weaver wriggled out from beneath the dead human.

A blood-curdling shriek echoed

around the empty street.

Raven peered through the side of the cart and saw the Dobermann, Davis clamped in its jaws, and DiTillio, Jock and Coltrane attacking it from all sides. It violently shook its head and hurled the tabby cat into the air and turned its attention to DiTillio. Jock and Coltrane retreated, and DiTillio sprinted towards the shopping cart. The snarling Dobermann gave chase.

"That's it, my dear. Bring that doggy over here." Mother Eve took aim and pulled the trigger. The Dobermann yelped but continued to race towards them. Mother Eve pulled back the bolt and took aim again. DiTillio raced beneath the shopping cart, and Mother Eve fired. The

Dobermann tumbled to the ground in front of her, dead.

Mother Eve got to her knees and rummaged around in the trolley.

"It's alright, Raven. It's over now."

DiTillio brushed against Mother Eve's legs, stepping in the pool of blood that had collected in the dust around her. She pulled out a box from the trolley and sat back down, pulling up her skirt. She tore open her tights to reveal the wound in her thigh. She removed a tube from the box and squirted a clear gel into the bullet wound.

"Lucky. The bullet went straight through. Though this is the last coag-gel. Never mind eh, DiTillio my dear, home is not too far from here."

She emptied the tube into the wound

and then pressed a dressing over the hole before wrapping a bandage around her leg. She stumbled a little when she pulled herself to her feet, grabbing hold of the cart.

"A little unsteady, but on the mend, our journey is almost at its end." She chuckled to herself and then stopped. "Oh! Davis!"

She turned the shopping cart towards the group of cats sat around the limp little body on the ground, and made her way over. Weaver and Jock sat in silence and Coltrane licked at Davis' face. The tabby cat's eyes stared unseeing into the sky, glassy. Empty.

"Oh, my poor little boy."

Mother Eve pulled out an empty sack

from the cart and limped over to Coltrane and Davis. She crouched down beside them.

"I'm sorry, Coltrane. I wasn't quick enough. I think I'm getting too old for all this." She pulled Coltrane aside. She scooped up the lifeless Davis and dropped him into the sack. She returned to the cart and laid the sack inside. Coltrane jumped up into the cart and hissed at Raven, then laid down beside his brother. Raven took the hint and jumped out. Mother Eve choked back a sob and wiped her eyes on her sleeve, leaving a dark patch on the dusty material.

"Let's move on then, time to go, not far now until we're home."

She leant on the cart as she pushed it

back to the road. Weaver and Jock walked silently beside her.

"Are all of those sacks..."

"Yes," replied DiTillio.

"How many..."

"Too many."

***

DiTillio sniffed at an old lamp post.

"Not far now. My old territory. I thought I recognised it."

Weaver, Jock, DiTillio, and Raven followed behind Mother Eve. Coltrane was still in the cart. He hadn't moved or even eaten since the day before. Just slept, or gently pawed at the sack containing Davis. Occasionally, he'd stared out of the cart, wild-eyed. Quiet. Any attempts to speak to him had been met with silence. Mother Eve had tried to make a fuss of him from time to time, but no one could get through to him. He was broken.

Mother Eve stopped and leant on the cart, taking the weight off her leg.

"Just over this hill is our home, a simple place to call our own."

Raven looked up the hill, the dead trees lining the road unmoving in the wind.

"Let's get going." Mother Eve started walking again.

"I'll be glad to get back home. I miss it," said Weaver.

"Aye. It's a quaint little place. *Our* quaint little place," said Jock.

"I'll be glad to see Mother Eve get

home," added Weaver. "She looks tired. I'm not sure how much further she could go."

"Aye."

The cats followed Mother Eve up the hill.

"This place was teeming with scavenger gangs when we were last here. I'm surprised we haven't come across any yet." DiTillio sniffed the air. "Something smells off."

"Everything smells off," said Weaver. "Everywhere we go."

Further ahead, Mother Eve had stopped again. The cats ran to catch up with her.

Laying in the road were the remains of four dogs and three humans. Blood and entrails littered the road around the almost unidentifiable piles of meat.

"Mutants..." muttered Jock.

DiTillio turned to Raven. "Be on your guard, kid. Seems getting home may not be as simple as we thought."

Mother Eve manoeuvred the cart through the mess on the road and they pressed on up the hill.

Raven watched the roadsides carefully. Anything could be lurking behind those trees. She had never seen a mutant, and from what she had been told about them by the others, she didn't want to. As they ascended further up the hill, the dust on the wind stung her eyes. She'd never strayed this high before. The dust got everywhere, even in the lowlands and the empty towns where she'd spent all of her short life, but now it clung to her fur like it had never done before. Raven really wanted to stop and clean herself, but the others continued to climb the hill, so she followed.

Mother Eve reached the top of the hill and froze.

"Oh crap..."

Before her, amongst the corpses of dozens of humans, staggered a hulking bovine mutant. Twisted horns caked in blood and meat sat on an oversized, misshapen head. One of its hind legs was gone, leaving an infected, bloody stump leaking blood and pus. Its whole body was a mess of bullet wounds and bite marks, though it was difficult to tell how much of the unsightly hide was due to wounds or its mutated form. Three bloodshot eyes scanned the area and fell upon Mother Eve and her gang of cats.

Mother Eve picked the sub-machine gun out of the cart and stepped forward as the mutant bull turned to face her.

"Beef Stroganoff it is then!" cried Mother Eve. She sent a hail of bullets hurtling towards the creature. Several found their mark, tearing away one side of its snout and punching holes into its neck and shoulders. The mutant beast bellowed and advanced.

"Distract it!" said DiTillio. "Give her time to kill it."

Raven looked at DiTillio.

"Now!" he cried.

The mutant struggled to find a rhythm as it awkwardly scrambled forward on three legs. Weaver and Jock ran at the beast, separating as they got in close. For a moment, it halted, looking like it might follow Jock, but gave up as Jock sprinted away. It turned back to its original target. Mother Eve peppered its face with another burst from the sub-machine gun, emptying the clip in the process.

"Damnit!"

DiTillio raced forward. Raven stood frozen. Mother Eve searched through the plastic bags and pouches in her cart.

The bull charged again, completely ignoring DiTillio as he ran beneath the beast's head and between its front legs. DiTillio sank his teeth and claws into the bull's scrotum. Again, the mutant bellowed, and began to buck violently. DiTillio was thrown out from underneath and landed deftly behind the bull. The beast spun around, enraged. Leaping forward, it thrust its horns towards the grey tomcat in front of it. DiTillio jumped aside and darted away.

Mother Eve emptied a semi-automatic pistol into the mutant's rump. Roaring, the bull turned to face her. She picked up a second pistol and started shooting. One of the creature's three eyes exploded.

Jock appeared and leapt onto the bull's face, tearing at the remaining eyes. The bull shook its head and Jock was thrown into the air. The creature slipped on the blood that was pouring from its wounds and fell to the ground. Triumphantly, Jock stood on its back, ready to attack again.

"Look out!" cried Weaver.

Jock looked up, but it was too late. A second mutant leapt over the writhing bull and snatched Jock in its jaws. It landed and shook its head violently, tearing Jock in two.

"Bastard dog!" screamed Coltrane, vaulting out of the cart and straight at the mutant hound.

"Draw it away! Let Mother Eve deal with the other one," shouted DiTillio, but Coltrane was already mid-air. The tabby tore away at the milky white eyes of the dog whilst digging his back claws into its jowls for purchase. He succeeded in pulling out one of the eyes from its socket, before the hound shook him off and sank its teeth into him. Hissing defiantly, Coltrane continued to claw away at the dog's face, until the hound bit down and Coltrane fell limp to the ground, his underbelly missing.

Weaver swatted at the dog's face and retreated towards a row of derelict buildings. The hound gave chase.

DiTillio had yet again clamped his teeth onto the bull's scrotum and the mutant writhed and bellowed in agony.

"That's enough, DiTillio," shouted Mother Eve. She pointed a sawn-off shotgun at the creature's head and pulled the trigger, spraying brains, blood, and pieces of bone across the dusty ground behind it. The bull's body collapsed to the ground, DiTillio pinned underneath.

Mother Eve ejected the empty cartridge and hobbled back to the shopping cart. She picked up her rifle and poked through her collected weapons and bags for more ammunition but found there was none left.

"Got one shot left with this at least, is that enough to kill the beast?" She cackled to herself. "Now, where is that fucker?"

Raven watched as Mother Eve shuffled away in the direction the mutant hound had gone. She made her way over to the bull. The empty shotgun cartridge lay next to the splattered remains of the mutant's head.

"Raven. Here!"

DiTillio had managed to squeeze his head and front legs out from beneath the dead mutant.

"I'm stuck. You and Weaver are going to have to face that thing by yourselves. Protect Mother Eve at all costs. She is the only one who can kill it. Do you understand? If she dies, we are all as good as dead."

"I understand," replied Raven.

"Then go!"

Raven made her way through the carnage littering the ground towards Mother Eve. She had almost caught up with her when Mother Eve stopped.

The hound stood between two of the buildings, a black tail hanging from its mouth. It threw back its head and swallowed Weaver.

"Oh, you're going to pay for that,

doggy. First Jock and Coltrane, now Weaver. It's time I put you down." Mother Eve lifted the rifle and got the dog in her sights and started walking towards it.

Raven watched the hound, but it didn't move. She followed after Mother Eve, and after a few steps, noticed something by one of the dead humans.

A pistol.

She meowed, and Mother Eve turned to her.

"What's that, darling? A gun? My clever Raven! Good girl!"

The hound turned its head and growled.

"Shit..."

The hound tore towards them, snarling. Mother Eve aimed her rifle and fired.

"Missed! Damnit!"

She hobbled over to Raven and stooped down to pick up the pistol. The mutant slammed into her, knocking her off her feet. Pinning her to the ground with its front feet, it opened its jaws and went for her throat.

Raven pounced onto the hound's face and clawed at its remaining eye. It threw back its head and howled, launching Raven onto its back. Unable to see, it went for Mother Eve again. As it brought its head down, Mother Eve jammed the pistol into its empty eye socket and pulled the trigger.

Again and again.

She stopped shooting when the pistol was just clicking harmlessly, and the dog laid lifeless on top of her. She pulled herself out from beneath the dead mutant and got to her feet. She looked at her blood-soaked clothes and chuckled.

"If only Violet and Edith from the bridge club could see me now! What would they think?"

DiTillio appeared and rubbed against Mother Eve's legs.

"Hello, DiTillio, my darling. Let's get you and Raven home, eh?" Mother Eve shuffled back to the cart and pulled out some empty sacks, then went to tend to Jock and Coltrane.

"You did good, kid. I'm proud of you."

"But the others... I'm so sorry, DiTillio."

"So am I, kid. So am I."

DiTillio and Raven stood and looked at the remains of the hound for a moment while they caught their breath. Then they joined Mother Eve by the shopping cart.

Mother Eve placed the bloody sacks into the cart and wiped her eyes. She sighed and then looked down at Raven and DiTillio. She smiled.

"Come on."

She pushed the cart into the field of corpses, steering around the gory piles. She stopped and checked in some of the buildings for supplies. She found a few apples and a turnip that had probably once belonged to one of the piles of blood and guts behind her, and she put them in one of her plastic bags in the cart.

"Not far now," she said. She walked

off at a slightly faster pace than before, humming a little tune to herself.

DiTillio and Raven followed behind.

***

Mother Eve stopped in the middle of the road and dropped to her knees. She began sobbing. Before her stood the burnt-out remains of a quaint little cottage.

"Is that home?" asked Raven.

"It was..." replied DiTillio.

Raven looked at the shopping cart full of sacks.

"Then it was all for nothing?"

"Not for nothing, kid. Life is a game of survival wherever you are. This journey ends, another begins."

"Where will we go?"

"To find a new home."

"Where?"

"Home is where the heart is. My heart is wherever Mother Eve is."

Raven watched as DiTillio walked over to Mother Eve and rubbed his head against her leg. She scooped him up and held him to her chest. She turned to Raven.

"Come on, darling. You too."

Raven had found home, after all.

MATCH TO A FLAME

By Kimberly Rei

The day they met, the world ended. Not their fault. Not precisely. Soulmate magic had been all over the news; the entire world was mad to find their perfect match. People who had been married for years were looking at their spouses with suspicion. If they were meant to be, where was the magic?

She hadn't wanted to destroy her marriage or anything else. But the instant she saw him, she knew. Electricity sparked, growing stronger as he walked forward. Maybe they should have noticed the air grow hotter. Questioned the growing energy. He smiled. She responded. Pinkies hooked.

ANDROMEDA

By Stephen Herczeg

She wakes. Eyelids flicker, stopping the blinding light reflecting off the crystal-clear waters before her.

A rattle as she moves her hands. She peers around. Chains bind her arms to the rocky outcrop she stands atop.

Across the bay sits her city. Its citizens line the streets watching her fate. Her parents stare from their imperial balcony. Memories flood her mind. She glares at her mother.

Foolish woman, she thinks. *Comparing my beauty to Aphrodite's. What better way to bring the wrath of the gods down upon all our heads?*

Hades stands behind the royal couple. A grin on his face as his plans come to fruition.

"Release the Kraken," he bellows for all to hear.

The seas begin to boil and foam as an unimaginable terror rises from their depths. Boats in the harbour overturn and sink. The bodies of fish float to the surface, dead or stunned. A nearby ancient rock formation crumbles into the waters, lost forever.

Andromeda pulls at the chains. Desperation replacing anger. The metal bindings cut deep into her wrists, bringing her efforts to a halt.

She turns back towards the palace. A pleading look to her parents. Tears form and run down her face. The queen buries her face in her husband's chest. His face remains stern. Unmoving.

Hades just laughs.

A new noise brings Andromeda's attention back to her fate. She turns and stares at the foaming tumult before her.

From within the turbulent waters, the first sign of the monster emerges. A massive four-fingered, webbed hand appears. Followed by a second, third, and fourth.

Then the creature's head.

A strange and repulsive mixture of fish, reptile and human features. Scales for skin with tentacles hanging down and thrashing with a life all their own. The creature blows a torrent of water and air from its enormous gills.

It stands to its full height. Towering above the outcrop holding Andromeda prisoner.

Its bulbous eyes stare down at its prize. It bends to gain a closer view.

Andromeda screams in protest. The Kraken withdraws for a moment, then reaches out with one tree-sized finger. A wickedly sharp nail snags Andromeda's dress and pulls. The fragile cloth tears free and is whipped away by the wind, leaving the young princess wearing nothing but a face full of terror.

The Kraken's face contorts into what passes for a smile.

Andromeda's eyes widen further.

The creature opens its hand and reaches forward for its reward.

Andromeda screams as the hand closes in on her.

Suddenly the hand withdraws. The creature stands to full height. Turns. Looks up at the sky.

All the city's eyes follow its gaze.

The king and queen see the object of the Kraken's dismay. They smile in relief.

Hades shouts, "No".

Andromeda looks skyward. Sees a small white speck fly out of the blue sky towards her.

She smiles. Her liberation is at hand.

"Perseus comes," she sighs.

First published in *Anemone Enemy*, Oscillate Wild Press, 2017

THE GROUNDSKEEPER

By Galina Trefil

"Go on," Arlo urged, pushing the spray-paint into Pippa's hands. "What's stopping you?"

Pippa Forrester blinked, swallowing, as her fingers reluctantly circled the can. She stared at the decrepit ruins of Castle Torwoodhead, which so many centuries prior had been built by her ancestors. "I…I…" she stammered.

"What's the matter?" Her young lover snorted. "You're not feeling sentimental, are you?" He grabbed the spray-paint away from her. With a hiss, the can released its contents. As Arlo branded a four-letter word onto the large, grey chunks of stone which the Forrester family had once taken so much pride in, Pippa hung her head. Her hesitation, she knew, was the very epitome of hypocrisy. She'd put tags on landmarks all over the world at this point—sometimes at Arlo's urging, yes, but plenty of other times completely of her own accord. So what if Torwoodhead was part of her personal history? It didn't deserve to be spared any more than the rest had…and yet…she still held back.

"Chicken," Arlo taunted, causing Pippa to resentfully stiffen. It was perhaps an exaggeration to call him her "lover." What was a better term? Convenience? Companion? A good-looking bauble to help her pass the time? Just another bored trust fund junkie, like herself?

It wasn't unusual for people like her to fall into drugs and the like. At least the two of them hadn't gone that route, she reminded herself with relief. She wasn't sure if she would call their landmark tagging an addiction. It was just the thing which kept them moving from place to place. And, afterwards, it gave her a degree of inner-calm to know that there was evidence of their existence all across Europe at this point. Vulgar as many of the tags they left were, they didn't wind up being ignored either. Ah, yes, people paid attention to them, paid attention in the ways which Pippa's parents never had, except when they'd been shoving their religion down her throat.

She had not been enthusiastic about Arlo's idea to come here. She'd known that he would merrily indulge in their favourite pastime and expect her to join him. She'd been too embarrassed to say that she wasn't sure if, as a Forrester, this was morally okay to do. Her living relatives never hesitated to let her know what a screwup they thought she was. Bad as spray-painting all of those other places had been, this just seemed to doubly prove them all right.

"Deep down, you're still just a goody two-shoes," Arlo challenged, nearing her in order to murmur into her ear. "Despite everything, you just can't stand up to Mommy and Daddy, can you?" Again, he held the spray-paint can up to her, his speech dissolving into a long series of fowl clucking noises.

"Up yours," she snapped, backing up and then stomping away from him. She retreated to the area which had either been the castle kitchen or dining hall. Settling on an ancient, wooden table before the fireplace, she took in all the other tags put up by random hoodlums throughout the years. Random bits of trash, in particular beer bottles and withered cigarette butts, dotted the room, along with charcoal from fires of previous explorers here.

Torwoodhead was not a castle typically frequented by tourists. It was too small, too broken. It was the kind of place that, sure, if it had some massive event happen there, perhaps modern audiences might deign to give a nod in its direction, but Torwoodhead had never made much of a mark on history. Instead, the most it could brag was it sat, remote and removed, as a sad relic of the glory the Scottish Highlands had once been.

Pippa's family had owned this castle

for several hundred years and, upon losing it, had suffered a wound to their aristocratic ego which had never quite been able to heal. Even after immigrating out of the country, the descendants still clung proudly to the knowledge that they came from the sword fighting lords and beautiful ladies that had contributed to the modern-day romantic stereotypes of Highland lore. Yet, at the same time, what was a lord or a lady without the castle to back their status up? Pippa sighed, taking in the damage before her bleakly. Almost, just almost, she could picture her gallant ancestors in this room with her right now, speaking in a Shakespearean manner and wearing stunning period costuming... What would they think of her? What would they think of Arlo, who'd just desecrated their once-beautiful home with the F word?

"Well, sorry, guys," she mumbled grimly to the dead, as if they could hear her, "I suppose I'm just a rude, entitled Yankee after all—just a plain old Forrester; not 'Lady Forrester...' But, then again, maybe Arlo is right. Why should I feel so crappy? I bet a good lot of you all sucked just as bad as the Forresters in the United States suck today."

"Forrester?"

Pippa let out a shriek at the unexpected sound of a stranger's voice. She spun on her heels and jumped backwards. Then, assessing the old man's threat level as minimal, put her hand across her chest as if it could shove back the heart which had nearly jumped through her sternum at his unexpected appearance. "Who the hell are you?" she demanded.

The old man blinked, looking her over for a moment. "I believe, lass, I should ask you that same question," he replied coolly in a brogue so thick that she could barely understand him. "You don't sound to be from these parts…and yet you speak the name of this Castle's owners. Do you hail from that noble clan?"

"Sure, um, yeah, I hail from it," she replied stiffly, not liking the old-fashioned term. "I'm just here to pay my respects."

He raised an eyebrow, and in the little motion, his ample wrinkles amply wriggled. He seemed to be evaluating her, which prompted her to give him a second-over. Despite the authority which he radiated, she felt quite certain he was little more than a run-of-the-mill hobo. His library green trousers and button-up coat were weathered, almost threadbare. The soles of his boots seemed worn down almost to the proverbial nub. White, unkempt hair emerged from a stained, overly-patched crimson hat. Truly, this stocky, ugly, little man propping himself up with a walking staff taller than himself looked like he'd spent the last twenty years sleeping under a bridge somewhere. And the smell that accompanied him indicated nothing to the contrary.

"You don't seem very respectful," he sniffed.

"Whether I do or I don't doesn't really

seem like any of your business," she quipped.

"It's my job to watch over the castle grounds, lass. It is actually very much my business."

Pippa couldn't help but glance at the mess on all sides of her. "Torwoodhead has a groundskeeper?" she scoffed.

"Aye." He nodded, eyes dark with utter seriousness.

"Well, you've been doing a piss-poor job of it!" she rebuked, tossing her hands up in the air. "This place is an utter craphole! I mean, would it kill you to pick up a bag or two of trash? Get a broom and give the place a good sweep? Or, I know, maybe get some weedkiller and have a go at all the damn plants coming up through the floor!

"Then again…maybe…you're not a groundskeeper. You're just a bum who's decided to set up shop in one of the rooms here because he's got nowhere else to go. In which case, fine. I'm not one to judge, but don't you go getting territorial about something that doesn't belong to you."

He shifted, visibly uncomfortable, and cast his eyes to the floor.

Pippa settled her hands on her hips, quickly ashamed of her outburst. "Look, I'm sorry," she put forward. "That was a jerk thing to say. Of course, this place is a mess… It's too much of a job for a…"— she caught herself just before calling him an "old guy" — "too much of a job for any one person," she finished carefully.

"It gets harder every year," he whispered, bristling with obvious humiliation as he took in the sight of the garbage between them.

"Well, hey, tell you what. My boyfriend and I have a tent with us. We're planning on staying the night here. In the morning, we'll take a couple plastic bags of junk away with us, okay? I know it's not much, but that should make your days up here just a little bit easier."

He looked up at her with the vaguest glimmer of hope springing into him. "If you came to help, that would be appreciated indeed."

Pippa let out a deep breath. "When was the last time that you had a decent meal, friend? Not meaning to put you on the spot here, but you look a bit on the thin side."

"I will dine with you," the old man responded, raising his chin somewhat indignantly.

"Well, ever so many thank yous," Pippa replied, a bit put off at his apparent lack of gratitude for her offer. Most geezers in his sorry position at least had the social grace to toss "God bless you" a few times or feign being overcome with emotion. This guy's expression made it quite clear he considered it a favour on his part, if not an outright imposition, that he would eat the food which Pippa provided. "Come on," she huffed. "Follow me."

She made her way back to Arlo, who had switched the one paint can for a second colour. He was merrily making his mark when they approached. Pippa looked back, noting how seeing this had turned the old man's eyes into a pair of outraged flames. His free hand clenched into a tiny, pathetic fist and, with his other, he gripped his staff so tightly that his already-pale knuckles seemed to instantly turn white. "I guess you were right," she admitted, to which he turned his head, full of grit teeth in her direction. "We're not the most respectful people. But so what? You're still hungry, aren't you?"

"Still hungry," the stranger finally, after a long and uncomfortable pause, nodded. "Yes. I will eat."

To her surprise, he didn't say a word about the tagging. His shoulders slumped, he glowered at the stones beneath him, and accepted the desecration. Poor guy, Pippa noted. He obviously loved this place, but in terms of protecting it, he didn't have a legal or financial leg to stand on. Fifty years back, maybe he'd have taken Arlo on over the graffiti, but age had stolen that option from him a long time ago.

"Hey, Arlo!" she called over.

"You changed your mind yet?" Arlo responded, before turning back to her. "Ready to get your hands dirty?"

"We've got a guest!"

Arlo did look now, instantly glaring and resenting the old man's presence even more than Pippa did. "Guest?" he questioned suspiciously.

"He says he's the groundskeeper." She shrugged.

"Yeah, sure. Sure, he does." Arlo stepped up to them, putting a protective arm around his girlfriend while even more intensely glowering at the stranger. "And just how did you get your job, Mister? Bet you didn't stink like that when you showed up for your interview, huh?"

The old man's eyes flashed, but he did not reply to the unabashed rudeness.

"What did you say your name was again?" Pippa inquired, trying to tone the conversation's hostile vibe down just a smidge.

"I did not say it," the old man stated coldly, "for you did not ask it."

Pippa raised her eyebrows, her charitable side wearing thin.

"Dearg," he muttered. "Call me

'Dearg.'"

"Dearg, huh?" Arlo huffed. "Guess you got stuck with one of those weird old Gaelic names."

"So many a man has, in the land of the Celts," Dearg quipped. "Would it suit you better, perhaps, if Scots spoke something else?"

"Stupid me." Arlo shrugged. "I thought that we *were* speaking something else."

"Much has changed." Dearg scowled. "And many of those changes have not been for the better." He glanced at the tent which had been set up beside the castle. "You may feed me now," he informed Pippa matter-of-factly, strolling off towards their makeshift shelter.

"What's with this dude?" Arlo glowered. "I don't like him. Why are you letting him have dinner with us?"

"He's just a grouchy old man. Come on. It's not like parting with a sandwich is going to be a big deal."

"He wants more than a sandwich, Pippa. The way that he's staring at you…"

After a pause, she couldn't help but let out a laugh. "You can't seriously be jealous!" she scoffed. "Of that guy? For real? Arlo, he needs a walking stick just to get around. The only way he's ever having a woman again is in his dreams!"

"That's not how he's looking at you. Not that way, but…"

"But what?"

"I don't know, but it's not good."

Pippa just rolled her eyes, approaching the campsite.

"Make a fire," Dearg ordered her instantly, lowering himself into a sitting position in the dirt.

"Why, yes, Master," she guffawed. "Hasn't anyone ever told you that guests are supposed to be polite?"

"I am not a guest, lass. You are. Or, rather, perhaps 'intruder' is the best way to term it. I lived on this land a long time before the likes of you ever set foot on it. For you, this is all a wee whimsical bit of fun. But not for me. Make that fire now. Do not force me to ask you again."

Pippa shifted nervously, obeying even as her first inclination was to tell the rude old jerk to get bent. "So how long have you been looking after the castle?" she queried as a small pile of flames eventually began to crackle at their feet.

"A long time," he muttered, his tone as weary as it was angry.

"What exactly do you do?"

"I clean up the mess, as best I can, at least. But you are right. Tis a difficult thing, in these times of blatant disrespect, for one so old as I to manage it. There is always more garbage, more disrepair. The things that take place inside my castle today, once, they would have hanged a man for it—hanged him only if he were lucky. But now men are left to do their worst and suffer little consequence for it."

"I suppose, growing up around here, it must be hard to watch a landmark fall into ruin."

"I come from the Borderlands," he muttered. "But the populace had grown too thick there for my liking. It is better that I make my home in a place such as this."

"But…isn't it hard? I mean, you don't have any electricity. There's no running water, no toilet. How do you even manage to get your groceries? And how do you keep them from spoiling when you do? Do you just have a giant hoard of canned goods hidden under the floor in there somewhere? And what about bedding? Don't you even have a blanket?"

Dearg scrunched his face together, obviously irritated. "That is a lot of questions, girl. I think not a one of them is your business either."

"I suppose you expect that we'll give you one of our blankets tonight then, eh?" Arlo snorted, approaching and plopping himself down on the ground beside Pippa.

"You are done then," Dearg observed, "with your foul mischief."

"It's called 'graffiti.'" Arlo smirked. "And, yeah, I suppose that, for the moment, I'm done. I'll probably put up another mark or two in the morning."

The old man's beady eyes narrowed coldly. "Feed me," he barked at Pippa.

"Careful with your tone," Arlo snapped in quick response.

"The Forresters were once an upright, decent family," Dearg challenged. "They were not ones to abuse the local folk. You would do well to follow their example, lass, lest you truly spark my ire."

"Dude, who the hell are you to tell her jack about her own family?" Arlo demanded hotly. "You don't know squat about those pompous jerks!"

"Arlo—" Pippa started, but he cut her off.

"No, I've had it, Pippa. This guy gives me the creeps. I'm done. Just *done!*" He turned his face to Dearg. "Now you listen up, you crabby old buzzard. You fly away now and don't come back until we're gone. If you get up in either of our faces again, I'll belt you one!"

"Arlo!" No. He couldn't mean it. Rude or not, this guy was old enough to be their grandfather, maybe even their great-grandfather. Arlo wouldn't dare lay hands on him, would he?

Dearg rose to his feet without a word, shuffling away while Pippa dissolved into a verbal torrent of anger.

"You just don't get it, do you, Arlo?" she snapped, once finished with calling him a plethora of unpleasant words. "We're in that guy's territory!"

"Yeah, and if we go scuba diving, Pippa, guess what? We're in Jaws' territory. That doesn't mean we have to try to cuddle one of the sharks though, does it?"

"That guy wasn't a shark."

"Like you would know!"

As it grew dark, Pippa sat in front of the fire, watching for Dearg's reemergence. "He's not coming back, Pippa," Arlo called from inside the tent. "He knows that I wasn't kidding."

She pulled some food out of their backpack and set it on a rock in front of the fire, hopeful that Arlo was wrong.

"You're trying to tempt that creep over here, aren't you?" Arlo snapped.

"What?" With both her tone and expression, Pippa played dumb.

"Yeah, you're trying to get that old guy to sneak up and run off with our stuff."

"That's ridiculous," she sighed. "I was just…"

"Just what?"

"Well, it's one of those dumb old Celtic legends."

"Yeah?"

"It's good manners to leave milk out

for the fairies on a stone."

"Give me a break. Since when are you superstitious?"

"I'm not. I just promised my little sister that, if I came here, I'd feed the freaking fairies, okay? Why are you making a big deal out of it?"

"Alright," he challenged. "Convince me then. If you're not tossing out good food to a stinky old jackass, then you'll be able to tell me the specific folklore that your nerdy, bookworm of a kid sister guilt-tripped you with."

"You ever hear of brownies before?" Pippa responded, cheeks flaming. "They're these little fairies that live in houses and castles. They help take care of them. They clean them up and—"

"So they're like the janitors of Celtic fairyland."

"Don't be a jerk."

He laughed at her.

"No, seriously, they take insults very personally. If you offend them, they leave your house, won't clean it anymore, and let it basically just go to hell."

"So…theoretically…if you leave milk on the stone out there, you can tell your dork sister that the brownies will be lured back and they'll get this place back to looking the way it should?"

"I guess so, yeah."

Arlo burst out laughing, doubling over slightly, and pointing his finger at her. He approached the refrigeration-free milk on the stone, continuing to cackle. He unscrewed the bottle top and poured it onto the rock. "Well, then, if you're going to feed fairies, Pippa, you better do it right. I don't think that they left milk out for them back in the day that was still factory-sealed."

She glared, but said nothing, disappearing into the tent. Hours later, in the darkness, Pippa awoke to a strange sensation. Warm. Moist. Something trickled from Arlo's body against hers, tickling her. "What?" she murmured sleepily, wiping at her neck, where the substance was drizzling. Blinking, she realised the wetness was rapidly spreading across her shoulder and chest, making her T-shirt cling to her with ominous stickiness. "Arlo?" She sat up. "Arlo, what the hell?"

Only then did she realise that a third party was inside the tiny tent with him. She shrieked as the intruder let out a ferocious, inhuman hiss before darting, almost springing, outside. She turned her attention to her lover, now frantic and panting. "Arlo? Arlo! Wake up!" She shook him and slapped him, to no avail. Scrambling in the dark, she managed to find the flashlight they'd set to the side. The sight of Arlo, blood gushing from his bashed-in skull, set her into a frenzy of screams. Behind his body, a few bits of brain matter had splattered against the tent wall.

Pippa finally got enough of a grip on herself to scramble outside…where she met the dark eyes of Mr. Dearg. He was crouched down on all fours, rather like a large wild animal, glaring up at her. Arlo's fresh blood soaked Dearg's hat, generously oozing downward and spotting across the malevolent old man's face.

"Why?" she sobbed.

His abnormally-long long tongue ran over the rock, slurping up the dried remnants of the milk. "I am no simple brownie, harlot," he roared at her. "I am the Redcap! Any Scot would have known, when they saw me and my hat, to run. Aye. All of them know well the method I use to preserve the colour in this pretty trinket atop my head. But, Forrester or no, you are a true American. You think that you can go anywhere, do anything, destroy and disrespect anything! I have been bringing villains like yourself to their just deserts from the time your people first stepped onto my island. You ken what I am saying, lass? I do not tolerate spray-paint in my castle! No, indeed, I do not!"

Pippa wanted to run or go back to screaming, but his gaze caught her like a chain. There was not a doubt in her mind that, once done with his milk, the creature would try to kill her as he had Arlo.

"You're a lot bigger than fairies are supposed to be," she choked.

"Half-fairy." He shrugged, continuing to lick. "Half-goblin. This gives me added height, so I may walk amongst mankind freely."

She swallowed, trying to remember the folklore. Beings such as this were magical, but not inescapable. "No matter my appearance, you cannot outrun me," he taunted her. "No human can."

"No," she whispered. "But I know what you hate, even more than people destroying castles!"

"What is that, pray tell?"

"Scripture," she replied, for the first time grateful that her family had been so religious. *"'Evildoers do not understand what is right, but those who seek the Lord understand it fully!'"*

At the Proverbs passage, the creature let out a cry, backing away from her like a large insect. Again and again she repeated the phrase, knowing that she could pull out a hundred more like it if she had to; if there was no other way to drive the Redcap off.

At last, capitulating defeat, he scampered away from her. "You saved your life, girl!" he taunted. "But it will not make your path any easier! That, I promise you!"

And no, it didn't. Pippa was found the following morning, staggering by the roadside, drenched in Arlo's blood. But when she told her story, the initial pity for her turned to condemnation and then to an arrest for murder. Redcaps were only a fable used to frighten children, after all.

Outside her jail cell at night, she would sometimes see the angry old sprite waiting, staring up at her barred window with beady eyes. He wore something now that, when he'd menaced people like her a thousand years ago, he'd never had access to: soundproof headphones that would protect him from hearing the word of God. "My hat will wear your blood," he vowed to her. She knew that it was only a matter of time before it came true.

FESTIVAL DAYS

By Raven Corinn Carluk

Once the weather held steady and all the seeds were in the ground, the small town held a festival to honour the spring. Neighbours gathered, the remains of the previous harvest were laid out, and joy was taken in the beginning of a new year.

Everyone who had involved themselves in the preparations was there to see the woman and her corgi walk out of the woods.

Goodwives paused in their work to frown at the stranger. Their little town had occasional strangers, travellers on their way between cities, or tinkerers with their wagons, but never a woman alone. Let alone one dressed as a King's Ranger with a corgi at her side.

The children were enthralled by the tan and white dog. Their folklore included corgis as protectors of the innocent and the lost, but none of them had ever seen one. The older kids tried to keep to their tasks, although much distracted, but the younger ones trailed after the pair, calling to the corgi. Gales of laughter rose when the dog glanced over its shoulder with a lolling smile.

Curious glances were exchanged between villagers, increasing in concern as the woman walked without acknowledging anyone. Strangers were one thing; a warrior on a mission was another entirely. By silent agreement, the goodwives decided to follow the pair, to keep an eye on them, make sure they didn't cause any mischief.

The pair continued toward the central green, ignoring the crowd of children gathering behind them. She was tall and wild, hair unbound, leathers worn and oft repaired, eyes focused on the square ahead, a pack on her back and a sword on her hip.

Goodwives began to follow her then, murmuring amongst themselves.

Menfolk worked on the green, erecting a maypole and preparing a bonfire. They chatted as they worked, grunting while they swung axes and shovelled dirt. No one called out to them, but they noticed the strangers and their growing entourage. Silence took hold as conversations and tools stilled.

She reached the edge of the square and knelt in the grass, removing her pack. Her corgi panted beside her, scanning the crowd with bright eyes. Goodwives called their children to hurry to their side. Men formed a cluster in front of the stranger, most still gripping their tools, more curious than wary. Even the town elders left their hall to come stare at the mysterious woman.

From out of her pack came rations and water, followed by several jars and a bell. She leaned back on her heels, glanced up at the sun, then opened one of the jars.

A horrendous shriek emanated from the cluster of elders.

Everyone turned to stare, the town leaders pulling back from the beast suddenly in their midst. Where the elder of livestock had stood, eight feet of burly monster slavered and screamed. Warty skin gleamed dully in the midday light, sickly and pallid, and large eyes narrowed in hatred at the leather-clad woman. It lifted its claws and charged.

Townspeople gasped and pulled away.

She calmly rose and drew her sword, her corgi snarling and racing toward the attacking monster. Turf flew from beneath the creature's pounding feet. Teeth flashed when it snarled, but she remained calm, posture relaxed.

Her corgi threw itself between the ankles of the creature, making contact before nimbly racing away. The attacker stumbled, snarl interrupted, and came to a halt just before colliding with the woman.

She took a step back, then lunged. Sunlight flashed along the blade as it sliced through the air. Ichor flew, and the beast collapsed without another sound. The corgi darted in and worried at its throat, ensuring the thing was deceased.

No one moved, and the few who spoke

used strained whispers. None could comprehend what had just happened, that one of their own had really become such a beast. Had she bewitched him? Had she wordlessly saved them from certain doom?

As quietly as she'd done everything else, the woman repacked her belongings, rose, and left the small town. No one stopped nor questioned her, and a sense of relief filled them all as she moved from sight.

Though they never knew her name, they dedicated the festival to the slayer and her corgi.

THE WITCH AND THE WARLOCK

By D.M. Burdett

"How are you today, Anne?" Dr Gardener, the lead psychiatrist, asked.

"You cannot win, warlock," Anne spat, grasping at her hospital gown.

"Dr Gardener is not a witch," Dr Jones interjected. "You're having a schizophrenic hallucination."

"Unenlightened fool," Anne sneered.

She saw Dr Gardener smirk, and anger pulsed through her body. Her eyes glowed, the room temperature soared. Dr Jones combusted into a fiery mass, his melting face screaming soundlessly.

"Naughty." Dr Gardener laughed. "But I will wear you down, witch. I'm winning."

With a flick of the warlock's hand, Dr Jones returned to his pre-spell state, none the wiser.

First published in *Curses and Cauldrons*, Blood Song Books, 2019

FEED THE MACHINE

By Monica Schultz

My hands don't belong to me anymore.

The real me had hands softer than silk with fairy-dust nails. The type that had never lifted a shovel. Now soot lines the cracks in my skin and callouses as thick as dragon scales cover my palms.

I miss my old hands, but these new hands are strong. Strong enough to lift me from the thin pallet, even though my arms have grown to resemble the spindly branches of a tree in the depths of winter.

Staring at my arms, I try to remember the line of trees that bordered our property. My memories bleach their bark of colour, transforming such a simple thing to ghostly silhouettes. Faint impressions slip from my grasp with every attempt to recall their exact shape. My vision blurs as tears cloud my eyes, reminding me why it's easier to forget.

What did Mother smell like? Was Father tall or short?

Without their photos, I am lost. I wrap my arms around me, shivering in my grimy shift. The cement floor turns my naked feet to ice even as I stomp in circles, pounding the life back into my legs. The sound stirs the beast in the cell's corner, a puff of smoke escaping his lips.

"Come feed me, Nine-three-five," Master croaks.

My mouth opens, an objection on the tip of my tongue, but I remain silent. Fresh fears of stinging lashes bury any thought of insisting I am more than a number. I hang my head, carefully shuffling my feet so I don't slip on the slick ice that coats the chamber.

As I approach, shadows cling to the iron furnace, shrouding his watchful eyes in darkness.

"You are slow this morning little one, perhaps it is time I found a replacement."

Tendrils of smoke creep from Master's mouth, curling around my frozen body, taunting me until I chock on the black air.

"Someone plump and fit."

The words burn my ears and spur my side. Lips pressed into a thin line, I swing the shovel overhead.

Crack.

The ice shatters under the shovel, releasing a puff of air that stings my eyes. Fitting my hands to the familiar groove of the shovel, I dig into the pile of coal. My arms strain against the weight of the first heap of the day. With a sharp flick, I dump the coal down Master's throat, listening for the hollow clank as it reaches the deep pit of the enchanted machine. Flames spring to life, travelling up the belly of the beast as the dragons deep within swallow their meal. Tongues of red flicker against Master's iron lips, chasing away any lingering shadows. A hum of pleasure fills the cement walls, moments before the remains of an unmistakable gas drifts from Master's gullet. Dragon's Breath—the simple solution to the global energy crisis.

Sinking into the rhythm of work, I lose myself to the repetitive motion of shovelling coal. With the constant addition of food, winter's icy grip over the cell weakens until the shovel is slick beneath my hands. Beads of sweat leave tracks on my blackened skin, cooling my scorched cheeks. I let my eyes drift closed for a moment, imagining the relief of a hot shower, the years of soot and sweat washing away to nothing.

"What have you done, Girl?" Master sputters, smoke cascading from his lips. Through the choking clouds of darkness, his eyes glow red with fury that sends shivers down my spine.

Coughing, I swat the smoke away from my face, "I don't know."

Master's eyes flicker, weakening under the constant demand from ravenous dragons.

"My chimney. Fix it. Now!"

I scurry to obey him, searching the cell for the only other tool – a scrubbing brush. With it clutched in my hand, I carefully climb the narrow steps to the top of the chimney, so the taunting flames won't singe my trembling legs. The iron rungs sear my skin as I travel higher into the poisonous by-product of consumed coal. Engulfed by the smoke, I squint to see the pale tips of my fingers, reaching for the chimney's crown. *There.* I clean with haste, using the blistering pain in my lungs to ground me against the unnatural sensation of floating within nothingness.

As my brush scrapes against the flue, knocking away the last of the creosote, a gust of wind lifts my greasy hair, cooling my neck. The canopy of smoke dissipates, revealing hundreds of children just like me, their faces a reflexion of my own hopeless and exhausted soul. I stare in horror as a child's legs buckle under the weight of coal, unable to bear the burden any longer. As their shovel hits the ground, their master flares to life. Flames leap from the furnace, dragging the child deep into its gullet, a rare treat for captured dragons.

A whistle resounds, hissing from every chimney in a synchronised call for a new cheap labour replacement to feed the machine.

My stomach drops to my knees, even as the smoke returns to conceal the evidence of child labourers. Yet I can still see more chimneys than an educated girl can count.

My knuckles white, I scramble down the ladder and stumble away from Master. His voice calls to me, but the thrumming that echoes in my ears quickly drowns him out. Memories rush to the surface; flashes of the concerned adult faces, warning of vile people who steal children, overlap with the assurances of my own parents. These things don't happen to children who live behind white picket fences. But it did.

I double over, bile rising in my throat. *Thoughtless, stupid girl,* I curse my arrogance to walk alone at twilight. To believe I was above the monsters that crawled the streets at night. Master was quick to correct such foolishness. Yet, somehow, I still thought if I worked hard then I would one day earn my freedom. Now I know better.

Blinking back my tears, I cast my eyes about the room, groping for a solid idea to settle my thoughts on. A slow grin creeps across my face as I notice the shovel at my feet. Snatching it up, I race to the door only to freeze before it. *What if they catch me?* The voice of doubt whispers at the back of my mind. My skin crawls with the familiar sensation of being watched. With my eyes squeezed shut to resist the temptation of peaking back at him, I square my shoulders.

If I die here, then I will die trying to escape.

Taking a deep breath, I jam the shovel between the wooden door and its frame, shoving with all my might.

Crack.

The splintering wood is music to my ears. I hold my breath, letting the shovel clatter to the ground as the door creaks open. The hallway is silent. I lift one foot, my stomach threatening a return of my meagre breakfast.

"HALT, Nine-three-five!"

My foot dangles mid-air.

"You will return to your duties this instant."

Heat laps at my legs, calling me to the safety of the cell.

"Families do *not* take back disobedient children."

I drop my foot, stamping out the flames.

"You stole me," I spit, my hatred leaking into my words. Only a monster would abandon a child to the guardianship of a machine. Fury boils my blood, churning until my feet are so light they are silent as I sprint down concrete hallways. My vision clouded by red, I pass countless doors without direction until I reach a dead end.

A wall, filled with countless rows of identical drawers, looms over me. Doubt snakes its way back into my mind, constricting my racing heart.

You're lost. They will find you.

I curl my fingers into tight fists, letting my jagged nails cut into my palms. *Think.* I scan the wall again, taking in the glowing numbers seared into each drawer. One for every child. Trailing sooty fingers along the wall, I hunt for my own.

932... 933... 934...

Slippery with sweat, I pry my drawer

open. A gasp of relief escapes my lips. My only possession, a book, is as shiny and new as the day I paraded it over to Lucile's house. I clutch it to my chest, daring to let hope seep into my soul.

My moment of peace is over, as my ears prick at the sound of distant footsteps. With nowhere else to turn, I retrace my steps. I cling to the stark-white walls as I scurry down the hallway, relishing in the stale, empty air.

My smile falters. Every doorknob I pass has the same brassy sheen and iron lock. I scan the witch-lights that line the roof, searching for the familiar blink of red eyes. *There.* They watch me, mocking even without lips to smirk. My lungs ache as I struggle to gulp down mouthfuls of air. The walls press in on me, shattering every hope of freedom.

Forgetting my resolve to check every door, I run only to skid to a halt before the last door in the hallway. The earthy scent of mud and rain fills my nostrils, drawing unbidden tears to my eyes. I hold my breath, taking hold of the only door strained by fingerprints.

Outside. Fresh air caresses me, lifting my spirits and easing my nerves. Under the darkness of heavy thunderclouds, I can make out train tracks curling through the mountains. My heart in my throat, I step out into the rain, towards them.

"HALT, NINE-THREE-FIVE!"

The words tear through me like knives. I ignore them and dart into the night. The mud squelches under my bare feet, splattering my skin as I struggle to find purchase. A single shot reverberates through the silent air. Before long, hundreds of fire-orbs join it, missing only by millimetres. The stench of burnt sulphur replaces every fresh scent. Adrenaline erases all fear, leaving behind only a single thought. *Run. Save your skin and get out.* With my heart beating a furious tempo, I lower my head and push myself harder than ever before.

A scream slices through the night, cutting through the blasts of fire. I am stumbling before I realise the agonising sound is me. Flames wrap around my thigh, licking their way up my dress. I flap my arms uselessly at them, thrashing my shift with my book. Rain batters my skin, beating my spirit to a pulp. Yet the downpour cannot control the wild magic of fire-orbs.

A beam of witch-light pierces the rain, lighting up my burning body momentarily. I squeeze my eyes shut against the blinding light, unable to face my imminent death. Yet, why does death sound like rattling train tracks?

My eyes fly open. My last shot at freedom is rounding the corner at high speed. Without a second thought, I tear my dress from my body, fleeing the flames. I hobble forwards, headless of the searing pain in my leg. Pressing my luck, I break into a shaky run and take a leap of faith.

Crash.

I land inside the train, my fall cushioned by bundles of thick unicorn skins. Panting, I sit up and inspect my leg. Raw blisters coat my skin. I gently draw my knees to my chest, hiding the growing curve of my breasts. With a sharp intake of air through clenched teeth, I survey my surroundings. Only the wealthiest of merchants could afford to transport goods that Dragon's Breath producers wouldn't dare to fire at.

Reaching out, I carefully open the cover of my book, gazing down at my good luck charm. A faded photograph.

My parents dressed in their lab-coats. My porcelain face flashing a dimpled grin between them, blissfully unaware that I stood with the founders of Dragon's Breath

Inc. I trace the letters inscribed on the back.

To our beloved Maribelle.

But I am no longer her. Nor am I Nine-three-five.

I am stronger, wiser, and in control of my destiny.

THE RING OF FIRE

By Ximena Escobar

Her deep, hollow incantation and the flames swelled. Orange reflections cast upon her eyes. One by one, slithering shadows emerged from the woods; they gathered around the campfire, lengthening tall into intangible human silhouettes.

Sian voiced her solemn utterance; small fire fragments severed from the flames, a firestorm cluster shooting into their centres like arrows igniting them—their human semblance appearing through the blazes.

She raised her arms and the ring of fire rose, uncovering their nakedness, their flaming-red manes vibrating. A ring of smoke like a halo spread, flames consumed by the cool, purple sky.

"Blend in," she commanded.

THE MAGICIAN'S ASSISTANT

By Kimberly Rei

"What's your name?" The magician flashed a bright and thoroughly fake smile for his audience. He bent down to hear the girl. Cornflower blue eyes stared into his.

She blinked, and for half a heartbeat, the magician saw blazing red eyes. She tilted her head as if considering.

"Esmerelda. Delilah sends her best."

The little girl patted the magician on the hand, then skipped down to her mother. The audience gasped as wildflowers sprang up behind her, chasing her every step.

They were too ignorant to recognise belladonna. Hemlock. Foxglove, with its beautiful white and purple bells. Nightshade. Low-lying jimsonweed. They all thought this was the magic and he was brilliant. But his hand burned where the child touched him, and his chest was beginning to tighten.

He backed away from the plants, turning to exit stage left. He very nearly made it. The last sound he heard was his audience catching their collective breath as he tumbled to the stage, blood trickling from his ears.

SEA-CHANGES

By Joanna Michal Hoyt

Three weeks after Miranda's plane caught fire and fell into the sea, Beatrice returned home from Miranda's apartment to the tall, white house on the island where she and Miranda had grown up. Her neighbours knew why she'd been gone. At first, they came by with casseroles to see if she was ready for talk or sympathy. Seeing she wasn't, they soon left her to herself.

She slept most of the first week. She'd hardly slept while she was in the city dealing with her sister's funeral, her sister's apartment, and the demanding sympathy of her sister's comrades, readers, admirers, mentors, protegés, and paramours. For one thing, everyone there kept late hours, and Beatrice had always been one to sleep and wake with the sun. For another, there was too much noise and too much unnatural light. Worst, when she wasn't busy dealing with the messes that accompanied being the next of kin of a freelancer who'd never made a will and whose bank book and check register were lost with her, or answering sympathy cards, or sorting through the debris of sketches, notes, books, cassettes, and objets d'art that crowded Miranda's apartment, Beatrice's mind crawled back into the same ugly rut: *Burned? Drowned? When did she lose consciousness? How far ahead did she know what was going to happen?*

She didn't stop wondering back on the island, but it didn't bite in quite the same way. She knew who had died in all her neighbours' families, and some of those hadn't been easy deaths either—Joe Caxton coughing out his lungs; Madge Siebert in and out of her mind, her family trying to decide how much medicine to give her and whether the pain or the delirium was worse; Billy Knollys after the car crash, badly mangled, dead before the ambulance came but not dead right away… It was part of what happened. That didn't mean she didn't hate it.

During the second week, she threw herself into her work. The goat fence was due for a checkup. The garden was a mess. Oh, not a total loss; she'd told both Ruth Caxton and the Siebert boys that they could pick whatever they'd a mind to, and they'd not let anything go to waste. They'd watered things, too, and done some emergency weeding, but there was enough quackgrass to keep her occupied during the daylight hours when she wasn't turning compost, canning tomatoes, or making pickles. "Such a peaceful life," Miranda had said. "When I'm too old and tired to travel and teach and photograph and write, I'll come live the pastoral life with you." And Beatrice had refrained from choking her sister. And then, after Beatrice had tended their parents while they died—helped, of course, by Miranda's wired money and sympathy—Miranda didn't have the gall to say such things again.

Beatrice shook her head, tried to clear those memories away, replace them with something better: Miranda, eight years old, already insisting on being called Miranda and not Mandy, coming in scratched and shining from a wee-hours expedition to the woods, a pail of blackberries in her hands. Miranda, thirteen, out in the sailboat, skimming over the water like a tern, always too close to the rocks, never wrecked. Miranda, fifteen, calling Beatrice to come right away, leading her down to the pond in the hollow just in time to see one of the dragonfly nymphs on the cattail stems split its brown skin and emerge as an adult, wet and smooth and shining, the sun flashing from its new wings. All through the days, the memories sucked and surged like the tide. In the evenings, Beatrice read the Book of Job aloud, pacing the kitchen floor.

By the third week, she'd caught up on the weeding, fixed the front porch, painted the tool shed, and cleaned out the greenhouse. That meant she could just about finish up her work in the mornings. Afternoons she walked by the sea. Not on the sandy beach with the kids playing and yelling, or in the cove with the jasper pebbles where the courting couples went, but out along the rocky headland where no boats anchored. Sometimes people saw her and waved. She waved back, then walked in the other direction. They let her.

She never met anyone in the little back cove on the western side of the headland. People didn't come in by boat because of the rocks; they didn't go by land because of the almost solid mass of blackberry bramble and hardhack. Beatrice went. The scratches on her legs gave her a manageable reason to curse. Staring out at the sea gave her a plausible excuse for repeating to herself the words that one of Miranda's friends had presumed to put in their sympathy card: *Full fathom five thy sister lies…* And if she sounded more bitter than spritely, there was nobody else there to hear.

Rich and strange. That was what Miranda had wanted life to be. What Miranda had been. While she was alive. Now…now she was ashes and bones. Wrong as could be, but not strange. Hardly strange.

Beatrice was grumbling in blank verse, perched on a pine tree that hung out maybe ten feet above the water, when she saw something pale breaking the water pattern. She leaned out to make sure of what she'd seen. Yes, there it was again—a solid thing tumbled in the waves; a large solid thing, with…

With eyes. With wild, silver-black eyes, darker and brighter even than Miranda's, in a silver-pale face. Eyes that stared up through the water and never saw Beatrice. Hands too, long, pale hands moving not quite in time with the swell and chop of the tide. *Drowning*, Beatrice thought. *And what am I supposed to do about it?* Beatrice could swim, but not enough to make headway against the tide, to keep herself and a dead weight off the rocks...

But the woman wasn't a dead weight, and she wasn't on the rocks; she was holding herself off them. She must be a strong swimmer. Then why couldn't she get her head above water? Was she tangled in something—seaweed? Rope? Beatrice's brain fumbled with the question while her hands peeled off jeans, flannel shirt, long-sleeved tee, tried in clumsy haste to knot them into a rope that would let her down to the drowning woman. She leaned out, thinking, *At least if they see this stupid rope, they'll probably figure out this wasn't suicide.*

The woman in the water rolled and dived, leaving Beatrice with a glimpse of finely turned ankles and long slender feet rising from a wild whirl of long hair. Long slender feet with webs between the toes. The hair was silver-green.

You're seeing things, Beatrice told herself as she scrambled back into her clothes. *Too much brooding about Miranda. Cracking up. No good.* She hurried herself back home, picked some pippins from the orchard, and made apple pan dowdy to take over to Ruth the next morning.

But as soon as the light came up over the water, Beatrice went out through the orchard and over the wall and down the road and into the scrub and onto the overhanging pine above the cove. Looking, just looking, not letting on to herself that she was looking for anything. Not until she saw the long, strong arms sweeping just below the surface. They were arms, they were really arms, with five-fingered hands, nothing else looked that way; they weren't seaweed or garbage or… or squid legs, or something. She was there. She was…

"Miranda?"

No answer. Of course. But the woman's face turned toward Beatrice. Whether she saw her or not was another question.

"I should have known better. Miranda…she was my sister, she was one of my kind, or at least she looked as if she was. But…oh, hell, I know better, I know better, she's dead, she's drowned, she's not turned into something like you."

The woman rolled away, impatient as Miranda would have been with someone else's grief.

"No, wait! Never mind me. You're the one that matters here. You…I've heard stories of your kind before."

The pale face turned toward Beatrice again. Well, what could Beatrice do? She started talking, saying something, anything. She told everything she'd ever heard, and some things she made up, about mermaids rescuing shipwrecked sailors. Hoping that it would remind the water-woman of someone her kind had saved? That was foolish. Shipwrecked sailors usually weren't on fire… Beatrice shook her head to clear the thought away and embarked on the story of the Little Mermaid—Andersen's version, not that ruin that Disney had made of it. She stopped halfway through, wondering if that tale might teach this creature that it was best for mermaids not to pay attention to humans.

Well, this couldn't be a mermaid anyway, she told herself; this one had legs.

Feet, anyway, and presumably legs to match them. Something else, then. A naiad, a sea-nymph. Perhaps that was less hopeful. She'd heard of such creatures comforting the souls of dead sailors, or mourning for them—*Sea-nymphs hourly ring his knell*—but not saving live ones.

But, of course, Miranda hadn't been alive… She resumed the story, stopped again, hearing the hoarseness of her voice. Then she remembered that the sea-nymph was underwater, that sound couldn't penetrate to where she was, that none of what she said could reach her. She swallowed tears. The sea-nymph dived and was gone.

Beatrice had climbed back down to the headland before she recollected that, apart from the question of sound being blocked by water, she had no reason to believe that sea-nymphs spoke English. She was almost home before she remembered that sea-nymphs did not exist. She shut herself in the kitchen, cried, and ate the whole pan of apple dowdy herself. During the afternoon she pushed herself in the garden, mulching paths, picking potato bugs. She was too tired to pace and read that night. She promised herself before going to bed that she would not go back to the headland.

She dreamed. In her dream, she looked through a net of rippling water at a woman's face. The bright eyes sought her own. The mouth moved. She could not hear the words, but something came to her from the woman, something like pulses of light, like a warmth moving lightly against the cold kiss of the currents…

Only then did she realise that she was not perched on a pine branch looking down. The currents swirled her hair and made cool eddies on her skin, and she looked up through the bright water. The realisation startled her awake.

She was out on the headland again at first light, though she had an hour to wait before the tide came in and the woman with it. This time she came prepared, with her Anthology of English Verse open to "The Forsaken Merman." She read aloud, shifting her eyes back and forth from the page to the sea-woman's eyes.

"Now the great winds shoreward blow, Now the salt tides seaward flow, Now the wild white horses play, Champ and chafe and toss in the spray…"

It occurred to her, of course, that the sea-nymph knew what the sea was like far better than either Beatrice or Matthew Arnold. But the sea-nymph lay still save for the rhythmic motion of her arms that kept her from the rocks, and her face stayed toward Beatrice. As Beatrice came to the part where the woman returned from the sea and sat in her home on land, singing, "O joy, O joy, For the humming street, and the child with its toy! For the priest, and the bell, and the holy well; For the wheel where I spun, And the blessed light of the sun!" the sea-nymph's eyes held Beatrice's for a moment before she turned and dived.

That night, Beatrice looked up through

the water again, and between her face and the woman's came flashes of a light less cool and comforting than phosphorescence and a warmth that was alien and hurting and yet somehow to be sought after. Night fell in the dream and she came again to the cove, swimming under the water. The woman was gone. The moon rode above her, silver and full. It called her, as it always had, but now the call was not only out to the water's edge but up, up through the barrier into the deadly places. She lifted her head from the water. The harsh air sucked at her, parching, so she had no choice but to go back down.

For the next week, Beatrice went to the headland when the morning tide came in, came back to work in the garden and speak to the neighbours when she had to, went out in the afternoon to swim. It was getting cold for that; she couldn't stay in more than half an hour and she came out blue-lipped and wither-skinned, and she never saw the sea-woman; still she went. Practicing, she thought. Building up her strength. Though she knew in the back of her mind that there was no swimmer on the island who could swim off those rocks, and she saw the sea-woman in no other place, however hopefully she spoke to her of beaches. Oh, the days had their frustrations. But she slept at night as she had not done since Miranda died.

Beatrice still brought poetry to the back cove with her, and stories about nymphs and mermaids, unicorns and dragons and every other wonder-beast she'd ever heard of, but she talked about Miranda too. Not about grief, not about the wall that had come between the sisters even when they could touch each other, but about Miranda's dancing, her laughter, her letters from faraway places, the day at the pond when the dragonfly emerged. The sea-nymph would listen to that. Once, even, she raised her arms so that one silver hand broke the water. Each day, her face looked a little more like Miranda's.

Then came Monday, the moon's third quarter and the neap tide. The water came fast but shallow into the little cove. Beatrice sat and read while the tide rose to its pitiful height and then withdrew. The sea-nymph never came. Beatrice came home too tired to do anything but crawl into bed and fall asleep at midday.

In her dream, she pushed herself toward the cove until the rocks bruised her and scraped her arms and she could go no further. Defeated, she let the ebb take her out into the deeps again, away from the warmth that had called her.

But there was another warmth growing about her now, seeping in from each cut and scratch left by the stones. Another warmth. Another strength. She rose to the surface, far from shore, and lifted her hand from the water again. The dryness hurt her still, but she could bear it. For one deep breath of water. Two. Three.

At the morning tide Beatrice went to the headland again. The sea-nymph did not come. The tide rose only a little higher than it had before. Beatrice told herself to go home. Instead, she crossed the headland and went down the meadow to the lovers' cove with the jasper stones. No one else was there. The water rolled the stones up and down with a noise like tearing silk, wearing them down to a softness that hurt her feet only a little as she waded into the sea. She went out with a dogged breaststroke, far out beyond the point, and then curved back toward the cove. Not too close to the point, to the rocks. Far enough out, maybe, to meet the sea-woman…

An hour later, having seen no one, she forced herself back in across the smooth stones, shivering with cold and exhaustion. She lay in the sun for a while, hoping vainly that her clothes would dry on her, before dragging herself back toward home. She made it as far as the road, where Ruth braked sharply, opened the door, and shouted at her to get in, what did she think she was doing? Beatrice protested that she was fine, but she didn't have the energy either to walk home or to quarrel with Ruth, who drove her to her door, walked her inside, and put her to bed. Beatrice fell asleep before she had decided whether to protest or to say thank you.

When she woke, her head was throbbing with heat and the rest of her body shook with chills. Ruth stopped in again after a while, took her temperature, scolded her, soothed her, tried to feed her, was refused, went away.

The next three days were like that. Beatrice slept in fits and starts, seeing Miranda falling from the sky with flames trailing like flight feathers from her arms, seeing the sea-nymph forcing her head above the water. She woke to silence or to Ruth's worried voice, shivered, slept again. Finally she woke to sweat and soft exhaustion, slept again for a long time, and did not dream.

The moon shrank and vanished before Beatrice was rested enough, and confident enough that Ruth wouldn't follow her, to go back to the tree on the headland. After that, she went on the morning and the evening tides while the moon waxed. The waters of the cove were empty. If she dreamed, she forgot before morning.

The day after the full moon, Beatrice stopped walking to the headland. The first light frost came, and she covered her tomato plants. The first real freeze came, and she pulled them up and threw them on the compost pile. She put Miranda's letters and her sketches in a box and put the box in the very back of the pantry cupboard. Her neighbours said she was doing well. She didn't care enough to tell them otherwise. Sometimes in the long evenings she found herself at the kitchen table with pen and paper, trying to catch the shape of the nymph's face. Mostly she didn't succeed at all. Once she thought she caught something of that wild yearning look. In the mornings she burned all the drawings in the wood stove.

The moon shrank, and the neap tide came again. Beatrice worked in the garden all day, mulching beds and hauling away dead plants, slipping inside whenever she thought she heard someone coming. At night she fell asleep quickly, slept dreamlessly, and woke in the small hours of the morning to the quarter-moon looking in her west window. She didn't hear anything, but she felt the summons all the same, a voice she'd never heard and would always recognise, calling from the headland, saying *Come*. She dressed herself in fumbling haste and went.

It was a bitter, cold night. Frozen grass crunched under her feet. Breath caught in her nose, her throat. She would have had to go back inside in spite of everything if there'd been a wind, but the air was dead calm. The stars looked small, close, and hard. They and the quarter moon lit her way well enough so she only fell six times on her way through the orchard, over the wall, down the road, and into the scrub on the headland. The summoning was as hard, cold, and clear as the starlight. Alongside it was her own hope, a stubborn warmth about the heart: *She'll come again. She'll come all the way., She'll come where I can talk to her. Once, anyway.*

She manoeuvred her way out onto the overhanging branch with aching care. *If I go to her, it will be on purpose, not because my hands are frozen.* She gripped tightly, leaned slightly, looked into the bright water. The stars snapped and danced on its surface. The glitter was bright enough to mask whatever lay beneath. Beatrice stared fixedly all the same; surely the sea-nymph could give her a sign, even if it was only a quick wave of a lifted hand…and if it was not the nymph but Miranda, if she'd come to herself again, then she'd be able to breathe air, and Beatrice could take her home.

Not that she'd want to be there anyway…

Now she might, now she knows…

Fool, fool, you always thought she'd know, she'd choose you, she'd choose what you chose, and you were always wrong…

Beatrice turned her face aside, scrubbed her coat-sleeve across her eyes to clear the tears which otherwise would freeze on her lashes. As she lowered her arm, her face still turned toward the rough fall of rock instead of the water beyond, she saw the shape that crouched there.

She had come, indeed. She was sitting there just above the water, her head thrown back, her hair aspill around her, covering everything but her face and her arms that braced against the rock. Her hands pressed into the stone almost as though they were growing there.

Not sitting, precisely – clinging to a vertical rock face. She must have suction-padded hands and feet like a tree-frog. Beatrice's stomach twinged. After all, it wasn't only the water that had lain between them; there was a strangeness—this was not one of her kind.

"Miranda?" Beatrice croaked. Her breath steamed in front of her, dimming her view of the figure on the rocks.

No breath rose from that figure's mouth. Beatrice held her own breath as long as she dared, watching; there was nothing. The pale face did not turn toward her, did not move. Was she dead? Had Beatrice lured her out of the water to suffocate? Beatrice scrambled back to land, took two stumbling steps toward the edge, wondering if she could climb down, if she should jump.

The figure on the rock shivered as though water ran between them again. Shivered and fell away, the slender body thinning, splitting, vanishing. And out of it rose…

Beatrice couldn't see what it was. It was so bright she had to close her eyes as it passed. Its heat beat against her face and body for a moment, then passed away. She opened her eyes in time to see it soaring high above her, dancing as it ascended, turning the foam to fire for a moment. It smelled like lightning, lightning and something else, something familiar that Beatrice couldn't place. She closed her aching eyes again just for relief, held them shut to study the dark purple image on her inner eyelids. *Not a nymph*, she thought. Not anymore. A dragon, flying. Beautiful, and gone.

Beatrice opened her eyes again and watched the darkness where the dragon had disappeared until she thought her feet might freeze. Then she marched home whistling "Cold Frosty Morning," put one of Miranda's sketches up in the living room, tucked the rest back into the box, and set about stirring up another pan of apple dowdy for Ruth. This time she would deliver it.

IN SEARCH OF THE PRINCE

By Christopher T. Dabrowski

The princess was looking for her prince.

Finally, she found him. At least she thought so when, in an abandoned castle, she found a toad sitting on a dusty throne.

She'd heard that it was enough to kiss him to turn him back into a prince.

She did it, and she turned into a frog.

Meanwhile, the toad took on human form; it was not a prince but an old witch.

The hag was glad that no one would stand in her way—and now she would be able to frolic with the prince trapped in a cage.

FREEDOM RIDE

By J.W. Garrett

Chills and bouts of sweat took turns as the boy shivered one second, then yanked the blanket up around his neck the next.

It's bad tonight, isn't it, Kevin? the boy heard in his head. *We can call it off—*

just for now. I'll come back tomorrow.

Kevin shook his head. *You promised… said you'd be here. Besides…I'm just not sure…*

Not sure of what?

You said you'd always keep your word.

And I shall.

A loud thud sounded outside Kevin's window. Under the moon's soft glow, his friend Sammie landed, tucked in his wings, and waited, his snout bumping against the window, formally announcing his presence. Slipping on a sweatshirt and wiggling into pants, Kevin left the comfy nest of his bed and crossed the creaky wooden floor, anxious to feel better as he always did when on an adventure with

Sammie.

Flexing and straining his shaky muscles, Kevin lifted the window on his second try, and after sliding into shoes, he crawled outside. A satisfied smile tugged the boy's lips, his efforts at freedom successful. Massive claws clung to the rooftop as Sammie edged closer, balancing, the wooden boards sighing under protest with each of his lumbering steps.

Sammie wrapped his long neck around the boy, keeping him steady as Kevin reached for the magical scales covering the dragon's hide. With the boy's deep breath, the essence of the dragon seeped through Kevin's body. A few minutes later, rejuvenated, and his pain lessened, he nodded his readiness as Sammie nudged him upward till he sat astride the massive creature.

"Where are you taking me tonight? Huh? Tell me."

"Ever been to the beach at night?"

Kevin chuckled. "Never. I live in Nebraska, remember?"

"Then that's where we'll go. Hold tight. You know the drill."

"Ready, Sammie!" Squeezing his legs tight against the dragon's rough hide, Kevin stroked the animal's long neck. "Thanks for coming to get me. The nights seem longer without you here."

Sammie canted his head and chuffed air. One foot hit the roof, then the next, followed by two more in quick succession. With a lurch forward, the duo dipped into a rush of wind as massive wings unfurled, slicing through the air, picking up the pace, pumping the two of them higher and higher.

Chancing a glance downward, the boy giggled. "Everything is so little down there. More, fly higher."

Sammie gurgled and spewed a tongue of fire across the night time sky, painting the darkness red, marking their way, and warning any creatures who might be in their path. "Rest, Kevin. We'll be there with the dawn. I'll wake you."

The cool air swept over Kevin, invigorating him as he lifted his face to the sky. His words came out in a jumbled rush. "No, I think I'll count the stars instead."

"As you wish," the dragon rumbled.

Throwing his head back, Kevin pointed. "Just look at them all… I'll bet there's a bajillion! One, two, three…"

***

The doctor finished his examination, pulled off his rubber gloves, and slid back the rolling stool to face Jim and Linda, Kevin's parents. "Your son fought bravely. But his body won't last much longer. The little guy's given it everything he's got."

The couple nodded in unison, a silent resignation weighing on their faces. The doctor's words were not a shock, but piercing nonetheless. This day had been coming for over a year. Their son just wouldn't give in. He'd promised them both that he'd never let go.

"Talk to your son. Reassure him. Chances are good that he can still hear you. Let him know you love him. Children have an incredibly strong will, hanging on despite excruciating pain. When you're ready, let him know it's okay to go." The physician shook his head, meeting the parents' gazes head on. "Kevin's got a lot of spunk. We'll miss him. Press the button if you need anything at all." The doctor dipped his chin and pushed through the door, leaving the three in silence except for the constant whir and hum of the equipment doing the work of life for Kevin.

Linda and Jim collapsed into a hug, then stoically pulled away and joined their son on either side of his hospital bed.

Linda wrapped Kevin's limp hand in her own, leaned down, and kissed his forehead. "Where are you?" she whispered. "Your dad and I are both here. Tell us about your adventures tonight. Take us along with you."

***

Their destination loomed ahead. Altering his pace, the leisurely glide of the dragon's wings shortened and picked up speed. "Almost there, Kevin. You with me back there?"

The boy blinked, his blurry-eyed vision focusing as he raised his head. "Wow! Am I ever. The sea!" Along the horizon, the deep blue of the ocean matched the darkened sky, but just at the edge where the sky and water met, a burst of crimson flared to life. A tiny kiss of yellow joined in, chasing the night. "I can even smell it."

The dragon gave a throaty chuckle, flicking his wings at the curious sea gulls, as he watched the birds dip their beaks into the waves below for their breakfast. "Hold on tight." Gathering speed, Sammie spiralled toward land and, hovering low just above the water's surface, played in the mist from the sea, Kevin's giggles echoing in their wake. "Want to stop and rest for a minute?"

"Can we?"

"You bet. Here we go."

Sammie sank lower still, planting his

giant legs in the ground at the final moment, eking out a long pattern in the sand as they skidded to a stop. Kevin slid down in a peal of laughter, pulled off his shoes, and ran to meet the rush of the waves. Their coolness brushed against his feet as the water raced towards him, then receded again.

"Well, what do you think?"

"This has gotta be our best adventure ever."

"For me too." Sammie curled his body around Kevin, nestling him close to protect him and take on the brunt of the wind.

"Can we stay awhile?"

"As long as you like."

***

The room was eerily silent—the machines off, the only sound Kevin's raspy breaths as their son fought for each gulp of air that wouldn't sustain him.

"I'm…here…the sea. Can you…hear it?"

Linda stifled a sob and adjusted Kevin between her and Jim. "I hear it, son," Jim answered. "I can feel the sun on my face too."

"It's peaceful here. Sammie said we can stay awhile if that's alright with you two."

Linda kissed Kevin's head. "Stay. We'll be here waiting for you when you get back."

Kevin snuggled closer against Linda's

shoulder, wrapping his fingers tight around hers, then suddenly lifted his head high, as if reaching toward the sun's rays. "I'm…warm, Mom, finally." Kevin's body shuddered as his chest rattled out a breath, and his lips eased into a smile.

TWO WENT INTO THE FOREST

By McKenzie Richardson

Austin slung his pack over his shoulder, excitement coursing through him.

"You sure you want to do this?" Clark

asked tentatively. From his tone, Austin could tell he was hoping for an excuse to back out.

Instead, Austin looked up, incredulous. "Of course, I am. This is the adventure of a lifetime. Who could pass this up?"

Austin thought back on the day, months ago, when he and Clark had been in the campus library doing research for a group project. They were wandering the stacks, trying to come up with a topic, when Clark pulled an outdated town guide from a nearby shelf. As he flipped through it, a slip of paper fluttered out.

It turned out to be a map of the forest. And on that map was a bright red X. Having seen his fair share of pirate films,

Austin knew that red X could mean only one thing. Treasure.

Everyone knew the forest was a dangerous place. Stories floated around about weird sightings and unexplained phenomena. Part of Austin attributed them to the college board's attempts at discouraging students from getting drunk in the woods. Yet another part was intrigued by the trees that grew so tightly together, as if making their own fence to keep out trespassers. As if they had something to hide.

Discovering the map had finally given him an excuse to explore the forest that so fascinated and terrified him.

"I guess," Clark said, his expression betraying his unease. Eyebrows arching, he looked over at Austin as though hoping he would call the whole thing off.

"You're not scared, are you?"

Clark pursed his lips. "I mean, it could be dangerous. I heard this one girl-"

"Yeah, yeah. I've heard the stories too. But that's all they are, man. *Stories*. Don't worry. We'll just go in, have a look around, and find the treasure. What's the worst that could happen?"

Austin noticed Clark shudder. Despite his bravado, he questioned his choice of words. Nothing good ever came of that phrase.

***

That night they set out, packs stuffed

with provisions and supplies, including electric torches, trowels, and plenty of water. "We don't know what we're going to encounter in there," Austin had said as though they were travelling to some remote jungle rather than the small woods behind a junior college. "It's best to be prepared."

Clark smirked at Austin's survival-show-ideology and followed his friend past the Life Sciences building to the boundary of the forest.

From where they stood, it looked like any other collection of trees, with fallen leaves and twigs littering the ground. Upon closer inspection, the two noticed little white bumps along its perimeter.

"What are those?" Austin asked, crouching down for a better look.

Clark joined him. "Mushrooms?"

The two exchanged glances. Their eyes traced the line of fungi along the forest's edge, each one of the small, pale caps spaced about two inches from the next. They were lined up like dominos, their fragile tops ready to fall at any moment and set off a chain reaction.

"Do you think it goes all the way around?"

Clark shrugged, never taking his eyes from the row.

"I've heard stories about elf circles where fairies are supposed to have danced," Austin went on.

"Do you think they're dangerous?"

There was a moment of silence while Austin thought it over, but finally he shook his head. "Of course not. They're just mushrooms."

With that, he stepped over the strange line and entered the forest.

***

As soon as his foot touched the forest floor on the other side, Austin half expected to drop dead or collapse in pain. When he didn't, he turned to Clark, whose brows were furrowed in their characteristically worried way.

Austin gave a shrug. "Seems fine. Come on."

He watched as Clark hesitantly followed, setting the toe of his shoe down first, then slowly adding the pressure of his entire foot.

"Where to now?"

Austin fumbled the map from his pocket. He squinted in the darkness for a bit before Clark was able to adjust the torch to illuminate the paper. They traced the path through the forest, noting the various landmarks.

"This way," Austin declared, pointing off to the right.

They hadn't walked long before they came to a pond.

"Woah, I didn't even know this was in here," Austin said, taken aback. His breath clouded in little puffs of steam. "Do you think anything cool lives in there?"

"Probably the usual slimy stuff. Frogs and snakes and algae and—"

A rush of water drowned out the rest of Clark's list. The torch beams swung across the surface of the pond, reflecting off the ripples marring its mirror-like flatness. Austin nearly jumped out of his skin when he felt a pull at his sleeve.

But it was only Clark, his startled death-grip snagging at the fabric near Austin's elbow.

The two turned slowly, shining their torches around, but only saw the gnarled branches of countless trees. Not until the final ripple had subsided did Austin let the tension ease out of his shoulders.

"Must have been a branch or something falling in—"

An ear-piercing screech filled the forest. Austin and Clark clamped their hands over their ears, but still the noise rattled around in their heads. Something grabbed at Austin's pant leg.

At first, he assumed it was Clark, fearful of the sound. But his friend's hands were held tightly over his ears, eyes shut. He shook his foot, trying to dislodge himself from whatever he'd been snagged on. When it held firm, he looked down, then stumbled back at the sight of a long tentacle twisting around his ankle.

The tentacle pulled with a surprising force and Austin fell backward into the muddy earth. His hands flew out, clawing at the mud, trying to find a hold as he slid toward the black water.

Austin's hand brushed against Clark's shoe. He made a grab for it, but his slick fingers slipped uselessly away. Luckily, the movement got Clark's attention, making him open his eyes. The unease in Austin's stomach intensified as he watched Clark's expression go wild at the sight in the water. Clark's body went rigid, staring just over Austin's head.

As Austin neared the water's edge, Clark stood in shock, at a loss. Austin cried out for help, thankfully finally sparking his friend into action. He clutched Austin's flailing hands and pulled with all his strength. He yanked Austin's arms like a deadly game of tug-of-war, but the thing pulling the other end was stronger— infinitely stronger.

With a final jerk, Clark's grip slipped from Austin's mud-caked fingers. Panic-stricken, Austin saw Clark fly backward, landing heavily on the shore. Austin screamed in terror as his trajectory picked up speed. He flung his head around, trying to spot what had him in its grasp, but his rucksack obscured his view.

With shaking hands, Clark spilled the contents of his bag as he searched desperately. Finally, he located what he'd been looking for and dived toward Austin. With a heave of effort, he dug the tip of a trowel into the tentacle, pinning it against the ground.

The creature gave a distressed shriek, then released Austin, who crawled safely out of reach. He turned around and faced the beast for the first time. His mouth dropped as he took in the appearance of the goblin-like creature with mottled green skin thrashing in the water. Long, sinewy arms poked out of its torso, and slippery tentacles stemmed from its lower half. Tiny, pointed teeth studded its exposed gums, and its large, yellow eyes were bright with fury.

With a final screech, the creature wrenched its tentacle from the shore, trowel still rooted within, and disappeared into the water.

Austin and Clark sat panting on the shoreline, beads of sweat dripping down their faces.

"What in the world was that? Some sort of mutated octopus?" Austin gasped when he had caught his breath enough to speak. Clark gave no response, never taking his eyes from the water.

"We could have died just now. That thing—" Realisation made the night seem darker, heavier, more oppressive. "What is this place?"

Turning toward the forest, they viewed it with new eyes.

***

They made their way around the pond, giving it a wide berth. It was difficult to navigate the forest without any trails or paths. Austin's stomach tingled with nerves as he considered the possibility of getting lost in the seemingly endless forest.

"We should pay attention to landmarks," Austin advised. "So we know the way back."

Austin was surprised when Clark only gave a short murmur of agreement as though it were something he hadn't considered. It was odd given his apprehension since they'd first set out on their journey. Austin shrugged. Perhaps Clark's mind was clouded with worry after the incident at the pond.

After a while, they came to a large, black rock. Its oily surface was as dark as grease, and it shone reflectively in their torch beams.

"Look at this," Austin said, stepping closer. The light bouncing off was blinding, but still Austin could not help but stare.

"What do you think it is?" Clark asked,

coming up beside him.

"Well, it can't be natural for one thing. It's too smooth. Someone must have put it here. Maybe the person who drew the map? To mark the way?"

Without realising it, Austin reached toward the rock, its surface so metallic, so mesmerising.

"I don't think you should—"

Before Clark could finish, Austin's fingertips made contact. The rock was cold beneath his hand. The icy surface numbed his skin.

When he heard a snort behind him, Austin's hand snapped back to his side. As one, they spun around to see what had made the noise.

Their torches only revealed trees and

plants, though there was a sort of fog around the outskirts of the beams.

They pivoted slowly, lighting up the rest of the forest.

"Wait. Look, just there." Austin shone the beam to the left and stopped. "Do you see? At the edge of the light?"

A slight movement betrayed something's presence in the darkness. It looked as though it were composed of spiralling smoke. As they watched, a vague shape slowly materialised in the mist before them.

When it came into stark relief, Clark and Austin both took a step back.

"What is that?" Austin stammered.

There was no need for Clark to answer. Before them rose the form of a bull made entirely of smoke. Its body swirled in puffs of whiteness, contrasting fiercely against the night. It may have been beautiful in any other circumstance, but here it was fearsome.

As they watched, the bull snorted, tiny sparks of flame shooting from its nostrils.

"I think we should run," Clark advised.

"Good call."

Without another word, they hurried through the trees, the crash of branches at their backs signalling the bull was in pursuit.

A stream of fire shot past Austin's left arm. He felt a sudden heat against his skin, his brain slowly registering that his sleeve was ablaze. In his surprise, he tripped on a root and came crashing to the ground.

As he thrashed about blindly, he felt Clark's presence next to him. He coughed and sputtered as dirt rained down on him from above. What was Clark doing, burying him?

Only once the flames had been doused did Austin realise Clark had smothered the fire. Clark helped him to his feet and the two were running once more.

Austin was surprised by Clark's quick thinking. He'd thought he'd have been the adventurous one on their journey and was a little disappointed with himself.

From behind them, flames spewed and the green foliage quickly caught. The fire raged and they choked on the heavy smoke. Racing along, Clark grabbed Austin's arm and led him through the blaze quickly consuming the forest.

For a second, Austin dared a look back and saw the smoky bull right behind them. He let out a clipped scream and pumped his legs faster. The shafts of light from their torches jutted chaotically, revealing a stone here, a bush there. Their throats burned with hoarse breaths and the heat of the smoke.

"This way!" Clark yelled, pulling Austin to the left.

In the distance, Austin could make out lights scattered about in front of them. The end of the forest, he hoped.

They came closer and closer, the bull right at their heels. Austin could feel the heat of its breath on the back of his neck. Clark yanked Austin in front of him, pressing him to go faster as he hung back.

Suddenly, Austin's foot smacked into something, halting him abruptly. It took all his effort not to fall. He pulled at his leg, but it was lodged in a root.

Clark raced up behind Austin and slammed into him full force. The root around his ankle snapped and Austin went tumbling to the ground where he rolled over himself.

***

Catching his breath, Austin saw the lights they'd just run through were actually pale flowers, so white they glowed in the beams of the torches.

Next to him, Clark leaned forward

with his hands on his knees, panting heavily.

Austin quickly pushed himself to stand, preparing to rush Clark on away from the bull. But pain seized his ankle. He whipped his head around to see the bull's location, but to his surprise and relief, it was no longer in sight. The plumes of flames were gone and the forest was dark outside his torch's reach. Examining the trees, there were no indications fire had ever touched them. No scorch marks, no burns.

He caught Clark's eye, confused and shaking.

"How did you know to go this way?"

Still breathing heavily, Clark pointed toward the white flowers. "Oleander," he wheezed. "It was on the map. A flower with a skull in the middle. They're toxic."

Austin shifted a bit away from the flowers, thankful of Clark's knowledge and a little disappointed he had not thought to memorise the map.

When he tried to stand once more, pain sent him sprawling to the ground.

"You okay?"

Austin squeezed his eyes shut tightly. "Yeah. I think I might have sprained my ankle, though." After a moment, he added, "Thanks for saving me. Again."

Clark helped him up and Austin did his best not to put any unnecessary pressure on his ankle.

"It's just through here," Clark said, indicating with his chin.

They stepped through the undergrowth, careful not to brush up against the ivory flowers.

***

On the other side, they entered a clearing and looked up at the sky. It felt as though there hadn't been a break in the trees for miles.

The clearing was perfectly circular, the branches of the surrounding trees not daring to stretch over its invisible boundary. A dark red, grass-like foliage sprouted along the forest floor. And in the very centre of the ring stood a lone tree.

It looked ancient, older than any of the other trees. Its bark was rough and dark, and its branches stretched up into the coal-black sky. Here and there, strange round fruit grew as red as fresh blood, peach-like in shape and size, although they looked rather shrivelled. Near the base of the tree, smooth rocks of various shapes studded the ground.

"We made it," Clark said.

Austin took a step forward, ignoring the pain in his leg. He was enthralled by the depth of the fruit. They were so odd, so haunting, but still, something drew him instinctively nearer.

"Well done," a voice called out.

Austin jerked, searching the clearing for who had spoken. He nearly lost his balance, but Clark kept him steady.

From behind the tree, a man appeared.

He had a grey beard and wore a long robe that brushed the grass around his feet, reminding Austin of a wizard from a film.

"Did you have any trouble?"

Clark shook his head. "No more than usual."

With one eyebrow cocked, Austin looked up at Clark, but the other boy did not turn his gaze away from the old man.

"Ah, very good, very good."

Austin found himself being guided closer to the man, closer to the tree. His head spun as he tried to piece together what was happening.

The old man gave a deep chuckle. "You look confused, boy. Come, have a seat. We'll have a little chat first before we get down to business. I see you've met my son."

Clark leaned Austin against the trunk of the tree, and Austin could not mask his surprise at his friend's betrayal. The man laughed again. "Yes, they all have that look when they find out. It never gets old."

Reaching a wrinkled hand up to a low branch, the old man selected one of the red fruits. He snapped the stem and held the fruit to his face, then inhaled deeply. The faint scent of fermentation tickled Austin's nose.

"You see this?" He dangled the fruit in front of Austin. "This is the answer to all things. Humans are such terribly frail creatures, not meant to live much longer than a century or so. For some of us, that is not enough. This helps us get around that pesky mortality thing. This can keep us going forever."

Austin's eyes widened. Then he burst out laughing. He couldn't help it; it was all so ridiculous.

"Okay, man," he said, turning his attention back to Clark. "You got me. I'll admit, you had me going. I didn't expect it from you, but this has got to be the most elaborate joke ever."

He made a move to rise, but the man held up his hand. "Don't believe in magic, huh?" He rolled his shoulders a few times, closed his eyes, and lifted his left fist to his forehead. Austin watched, his expression skeptical.

After a few seconds, the man lowered his hand to chin level. Then, with a snap of his fingers, opened his eyes.

In an instant, Austin felt the pain in his ankle subside. The scratches on his hands and arms receded. His jaw dropped, and he quickly snapped it shut again.

He rolled out his ankle, feeling the freedom of his moments. "How did you do that?"

The old man chuckled. "A mage as old as I am picks up a trick or two over the centuries."

Austin stood straighter, eyeing him thoughtfully. "So why am I here? Why did Clark bring me?"

Clark stood quietly, observing all that came to pass.

"My son and I have our tasks. I guard the tree and he ventures into the outside world. You see, magic always comes at a price. He brings me what I need to continue our way of life."

Clark remained motionless, as though he were made of stone.

"So, he lured me here? Why?"

The mage raised the wrinkled fruit still in his hands. "Because of this."

The sickly-sweet smell of rotting fruit made Austin gag. It was so powerful now, almost unbearable.

"The Forever Fruit." The mage's eyes shone as he spoke, an otherworldly light brightening his features. He took Austin's hand and set the fruit in his palm.

"As I said, magic always comes at a price. This tree can't grow on its own. Most plants merely need light, water, and air. But this tree is special. This tree needs something more to grow its miraculous fruit."

A twisted smile crept across the man's face and he squinted at Austin, who quickly shifted his gaze to the ground. When he did, he noticed something strange about the rocks. They were so round and smooth, a pale yellowish colour, almost white. He leaned his head forward, trying to get a better look without being too obvious.

One stone in particular had an odd familiarity to it. It poked out of the dirt, a large hole in one side. Further along its surface, he could make out a few bumps. They looked almost like…teeth.

Realisation hit him all at once, and he pressed himself back against the tree. The bark scraped at his skin as his fingers dug in. They weren't rocks at all but bones, the skull recognisably human.

The man laughed again. "Ah, a smart boy. I see you've figured it out, then? Yes, this tree needs fresh blood to bear its fruit. As you can see, it has been a while since it last feasted and its fruit has begun to rot. It needs a new food source to produce more fruit. I assume you're smart enough to connect the rest."

Austin stared in horror at the bone near his foot. Bile rose in his throat, and he shook his head to clear the morbid images from his mind.

He swallowed hard, then turned his attention to Clark.

"And you're just going to let him do

this? I thought we were friends."

Clark made no movement, staring ahead, as still as a statue.

"Don't feel too bad, my boy," the man said condescendingly. "He's tricked many here before you. He has a knack for gaining others' trust."

Austin's jaw clenched.

"Now, to get on with business." He pulled a long knife from somewhere in the folds of his robes. "Sorry to have to do this. It really has been nice chatting with you. But I'm afraid there just isn't time." He pursed his lips, considering. "Well, I suppose for me there is. I've got all the time in the world. You, on the other hand…"

He took a step closer and raised the blade.

***

Thinking quickly, Austin kicked out with his newly-healed leg. His shoe made contact with the man's knee, sending a loud cracking noise through the clearing.

The mage buckled, rage burning in his eyes.

"Get him!" he screamed to Clark.

Clark did not hesitate. He lunged at Austin, who was making a clumsy effort across the crimson grass. With one sweep of his hand, he snatched Austin by the back of the collar. He lifted him as easily as a stray cat, dangling him above the ground with unexpected strength. Gone was the timid boy Austin thought he'd known so well. This was someone else entirely.

As Austin stared down into Clark's blank face, his mind filled with memories. Late-night study sessions, toasting marshmallows over the Bunsen burners in the chemistry lab, drinking far too many cans of cheap beer until Clark had fallen down the stairs.

An idea sparked in Austin's brain. He watched Clark as he stood motionless, suspending him in the air.

"Kill him!" the old mage roared. He sent the knife toward Clark on a puff of air, and Clark caught it without breaking eye contact.

He raised the knife, pausing momentarily. His eyes took on a hint of sadness, barely detectable in the darkness.

Austin took his chance. He sent his right hand flying, punching out at Clark. It landed squarely on the shoulder Clark had injured during his drunken tumble. He winced and lowered Austin slightly, the knife dropping from his grip. Austin lashed out again. The shoulder had never healed quite right, and Austin was glad of the slight advantage.

The third time Austin struck, Clark dropped him to the ground. Austin landed on his feet and made for the forest bordering the clearing.

Before he had gone too far, Clark lunged to grab him. Austin dodged his fingers, sending another fist in Clark's direction. This time it hit Clark square in the face. He sputtered, then fell backward, his body rigid, blood gushing from his nose and splattering his chest.

There was a sickening smacking noise when he hit the ground, his head slamming against the skull protruding from the grass.

Austin looked back toward the person he had once called friend.

A slithering sound filled his ears and snake-like roots tangled around Clark's body. They entwined and enveloped him, pulling him down into the loose soil.

The mage limped forward, favouring his wounded knee. He stood over Clark's rapidly disappearing body, then shifted his gaze toward Austin.

Austin expected him to cast some sort of spell then, or chase him or yell or something. But instead, the mage just stood there. He nodded once, then glanced down at his son.

Austin did not wait to see what became of Clark. He turned toward the trees and ran as fast as he could. He flew through the poisonous plants, past the large black rock, and around the pond.

Just behind him, he felt a presence chasing him through the darkness. He kept running, doing his best to avoid the branches and rocks that jutted out to trip him.

Before long, he saw lights in front of him. Not the strange, otherworldly lights of the forest. Actual lights. From a building or a car or a streetlight. Something real, something human.

With the last of his strength, he

propelled himself out of reach of the trees. He saw the white dots of the fairy circle and leapt across, careful not to decapitate any of the soldiers in the protective line that kept the forest at bay.

When he reached the other side, he didn't have enough strength to slow his momentum. Instead, he fell to the ground and rolled a few times, finally coming to a stop, back against the green grass, panting heavily. He gasped for air in the cold night and looked up at the sky.

It was just as dark as it had been when he and Clark had entered the forest, as if no time had passed at all. But that couldn't be. They'd been in there for so long—a lifetime it seemed.

Austin lifted his left hand to pull out

his phone, but found it was already occupied. He brought it to his face and instantly recognised the stomach-churning sweetness of the Forever Fruit. It oozed in his hand, coating his palm in sticky syrup.

He almost laughed. So, he'd found the treasure after all.

He took a bite of the sweet-smelling fruit, feeling its fizzy essence burst in his mouth. He continued to eat until he came to the heart of the fruit. It tasted harsh, bitter, acidic, and seemed to pulsate at his touch. He let it fall to the grass at his side after sucking it dry of juice.

Then, he headed back to his car, contemplating whether he'd be able to shower when he got home or just collapse into bed.

As his silhouette disappeared from view, peace returned. The continuous line of mushrooms stretched along the border, white, luminous, and unbroken.

Just beyond them sat the red seed of the Forever Fruit, gleaming in the moonlight.

And then all was quiet, the night two went into the forest and something else came out.

BANEPYRE AND BITEWIND

By Shawn M. Klimek

Through a window or a keyhole, there
would seem not much to see:
Just two old men playing checkers,
smoking pipes and drinking tea.

But up close, the tea is purplish and there's
foam atop the water,
And the pipe smoke hovers oddly, and its
odour's even odder;

And the checkers that they're using would
leave anyone agog
Who observed one jumping by itself and
croaking like a frog!

For you see, both men are wizards: former
rivals but now friends,
Who've agreed the fate of magic on their
strategy depends.

Of the pair, Bitewind is taller, and he likes
to tease his hair,
So that sometimes it's mistaken for a cat
that's had a scare.

Banepyre's fat and a curmudgeon: always
scowling, ever snacking.
He keeps pickles in his boot cuffs for those
times his host is lacking.

"It's an outrage!" Banepyre mumbled as he
was so fond of doing
That his host heard every syllable, despite
his pipe and chewing.

Bitewind nodded in agreement. He knew well which words would follow

Once his guest had puffed his pipe and gulped some tea to help him swallow.

"*Damn* tradition," Bitewind prompted, "*and what all those fools believe.*"

Then to emphasise his eyebrows, wiped his glasses on his sleeve.

"That's exactly what I'm saying!" Banepyre said and shook his fist.

"When their archmage is in error, noble wizards must resist!"

"Errors cannot be allowed," his host concurred. "That much is clear,
"And on that subject, shouldn't this red checker piece be over here?"

"Oh? Ah!" said Banepyre simply. "Beg your pardon. Damn these sleeves!
"But let us now return to what our fool archmage believes."

"Had that dying race of wizards from which all of us descend,
"Never deigned to breed with humans, magic would have met its end."

"Sadly true," acknowledged Bitewind.

"Here we both see eye to eye.

"And it's obvious our secrets must be shared before we die!"

"But to fewer wizards would be best!" Banepyre complained, excited.

"Since the power of our bloodline fades each time it is divided,"

"There is the rub," lamented Bitewind.

"With exceptions, I must say,

"By and large, each new apprentice furthers wizardry's decay."

Here, both paused to nod then shake their heads—a massive pair:
Banepyre's thick-jowled, double-chinned;
Bitewind's grey, bushy hair.

The heavier mage said to his host, "I must apologise.
"My passions are so great, sometimes, they catch me by surprise."

"No need!" deflected Bitewind, but he recognised his cue.
Banepyre's passions made him peckish.
"Shall I bring one cake, or two?"

The portly mage held up two fingers. "And,
as long as you are up,
"More tea. I'm parched from shouting and
I've drained another cup."

Bitewind entered his kitchen, where he was
surprised to see
His apprentice with a platter stacked with
cakes and steaming tea.

"Never mind us," offered Bitewind. "Had
I realised you were home,
"I'd have sent you on an errand to search
for my wand and comb."

The apprentice meekly answered, "I once
saw them in your hat,"
"But of course!" said Bitewind brightly.
"There's your errand. Go find that."

Returning early with the platter, Bitewind
thought he caught a snatch
Of Banepyre altering the game board—but
just how, he didn't catch.

"Refreshed refreshments," he announced,
his tone sharply accusing.
Red-handed, Banepyre simply said,
"You'll find the truth amusing:"

"I am not a tidy eater: I use both hands—mostly thumbs.

"So, you see, I'm not a cheater; I was merely brushing crumbs!"

Bitewind considered this, then laughing, said, "You *are* a slob,"

"But frivolity, food and friendship must come second to our *job*..."

"Safeguarding sacred wizardry from its spiralling decline.

"To wit: witless apprentices. Shall we start with yours or mine?"

Banepyre's face resumed its norm: a shadowed, scowling mask.

"These lads look up to us," he frowned, "which complicates our task."

"To willfully betray such trust is challenging to scruple.

"Therefore, let's start with Witherly, your own pathetic pupil."

"We could," admitted Bitewind, as he refilled Banepyre's tea.

"And yet someone must inherit magic for posterity."

"And since Witherly is dedicated, obedient and bright,

"I thought, why not instead start with your sad Netherwight."

At these words, Banepyre bristled, and his tone began to cool.

"Both are witless, that's established, *yet my own's the lesser fool.*"

"My Netherwight's hardworking, innovative, and ambitious.

"So, to slight him over Witherly would seem unjust and pernicious."

Bitewind's countenance grew grave, and his hands began to tremble,
And his hair increasingly resembled what such things resemble:

Roaring lions or dandelions, or tumbleweeds in swells,
Or bushes shook by stomping giants (or plain bush-shaking spells).

Banepyre could not but notice that his host set down the platter
In a fashion quite the opposite of when nothing is the matter.

Nor could Banepyre fail to see what his
host had so far missed:
An accusing, floating finger jutting from a
phantom fist.

The finger aimed at Banepyre, who in
outrage and alarm,
Shrieked, "What is this, Bitewind? Do you
mean to do me harm?"

Having asked himself that very thing, just
prior to this confusion,
Bitewind scarcely had to ponder before
voicing his conclusion.

But as he turned to speak, the spectral
gesture caught his glance,
Interrupted next by Witherly, before he got
the chance.

"Please forgive me, Master Wizards,"
Witherly beseeched the pair.
"That hand was made for errands but
prefers a comfy chair."

Bitewind was embarrassed, on not just the
lad's behalf.
That his argument was lost seemed
reinforced by Banepyre's laugh.

"Would you still trust," Banepyre challenged, "The dire future of our craft

"To such witless hands as those three?" At this joke, again he laughed.

Bitewind glowered at his student. "I gave you no tasks in this room!

"Your neglect and magic blunders have together sealed your doom."

Feeling awkward in his triumph and ill-at-ease beneath the hand,

Banepyre realised it was time to go and made a move to stand.

But no sooner had he lifted his wide rump
into the air
Then the apparition fingered Bitewind's
hat upon the chair.

Witherly was first to notice, but before he
could exclaim,
Bitewind signalled him and said, "Tut, tut.
I see you weren't to blame."

Then to Banepyre, Bitewind levelled a
recriminating gaze.
"I think somebody's entitled to apologies
and praise."

"Do you mean to say this spell worked?
This spell *cast by an apprentice*?
Bitewind nodded. "Well, in that case, I'll
admit, it is momentous."

Banepyre's face displayed the struggle
going on inside his brain.
Its convulsions rendered every shape and
hue of psychic pain.

"Very well!" at last he shouted. "I
reluctantly concede,
"That your Witherly is worthier to answer
Magic's need."

"It's a bitter pill to swallow, to betray my
student's trust,
"But since magic's very fate's at stake, I
accept now, that I must."

"When Netherwight asks for knowledge, I
will let him know his lack;
"When for guidance, I shall guide him to
despair and never back."

"I will discourage his ambitions, by
instilling him with doubt.
"For the sacred sake of wizardry, we will
weed weak wizards out!"

Bitewind gave his wizard friend a sympathetic pat.

"You have your wand and pipe?" he asked. "I'll grab your cloak and hat."

There was once an evil wizard, filled with malice, spite, and scorn.

And we here conclude the story of how he was made, not born.

THE PRINCESS BRIBE

By John H. Dromey

The Dark Knight stormed into the ancient castle, brandishing his good looks. That was his intent, anyway. In his haste— and in full armour—he put his foot down a smidgeon harder than he should have. His metal-clad metatarsal bone and its two hundred close companions made quite an impact. The knight was still about three paces shy of the entrance to the king's stronghold when there was a prolonged ripping sound, followed by a loud splash.

Informed of the mishap, the king was almost apologetic. "Of all the wretched luck," he said. "I've been meaning to have my steward replace that rotten board in the drawbridge."

"What should we do for the knight?" a page asked.

"Alas, there's nothing more that can be done for him, but perhaps we can do something for ourselves. Take a grappling hook and a winch, and see if you can at least retrieve his armour before it has a chance to rust."

"You told me to stay away from the serving wenches, sire."

"So I did. Get the cook to help you."

Some considerable time later, the begrimed knight showed up in the royal chambers for his audience with the reigning monarch.

"You are, I presume, the Black Knight," the king said. "You're early."

"No, my liege, I am the Dark Knight."

"It's small wonder I failed to perceive such a fine distinction in the hue of your armour. Your coat of mail appears to me as black as night-time in a dungeon."

"I assure you, sire, I am indeed the Dark Knight."

"You're late, then, or rather, you are

the late Dark Knight, the shade of your former self, for surely you could not have survived a plunge in the moat. This is my first daylight encounter with a ghost."

"I am still quick."

"Are you suggesting that I am slow of wit?"

"I mean I'm alive. I managed to keep my head above water, or rather, above the sludge which stained my armour."

"Ah, yes. There's a silt problem with the moat, but that's not why I put out a call for champions. Rid my kingdom of the wicked dragon that threatens our eastern borders, and I will give you my eldest daughter's foot."

"What about her hand?"

"Sorry. That's already been spoken for

by the White Knight."

"Eccch! Supposing I were interested in your daughter's foot, how is that even possible?"

"Alas and alack, her wedding plans are falling apart, and so, too, is the princess," the king said. "She's a zombie."

First published in *three minute plastic*, 2012

FADE TO WHITE

By Ximena Escobar

The dread of constant eyes. Constant eyes watching me. For once I wasn't afraid; the leaves rustled, and I faced them.

I saw those eyes were vulnerable. A light that I recognised. A flicker wrapped in fear—something we had in common.

A beautiful distress in those eyes; seeing orbs surrounded by darkness.

The splashes of black between the branches moved. It hurt like a rupture to see them become one line, separate, shape into the outline of wings as her glowing eyes surged and her form stepped out from the trees into the light of day. Autumn leaves turned to feathers, falling like a dead bride's trail as she neared me.

I was severed too. Severed from my moment's completion. There was never going to be an embrace. The pearlescence of her skin dimmed into the dullness of bone, wings bare like white winter branches.

"You've killed me," she said in her

silence, her silhouette reflected on the pool of blood around me, the dagger still inside me. "I only wish you'd done it sooner."

A tear stirred the crimson puddle, whiteness rising from the darkest depths of crimson.

"I never meant to hurt you," I said.

"I never meant to frighten you."

Guardian angel disappearing, we faded to white together.

DEATHBIRTH

By Christopher T. Dabrowski

I remember a bright, blinding light. A feeling of immeasurable happiness and all-embracing love. But then I was I was awakened from death, grasped by two luminous creatures, and yanked backwards, sucked into a dark tunnel. The wonderful light moved further and further away until it completely disappeared... Paradise lost. I did not feel any fear; everything was delightfully neutral.

When we flew down to the ground, the creatures released me. I was next to my own body. I just stood there, watching. At first, I did not care at all—as if I was viewing some boring museum piece—but then something made me re-enter my body, and my feelings changed. I woke to life. I was lying on the pavement, feeling as if I had an enormous weight on my chest. I slowly came to my senses; this was my deathbirth—I returned to the world with a massive heart attack.

In one moment, I saw my whole life play out in front of me. The strangest thing was, I'd known every detail since I was a small child. I'd understood, for some forty or fifty years, that I would be a librarian, and my dreams of being a real writer would never come true. What cruelty! A man is born to this world and already knows that he will be a nobody; that his future will bear a lot of boring years full of disappointment and unfulfilment.

Everyone must live to his unbirth; mine will be in seventy-eight years, three months, and five days. For some period in life, the passing of years is a blessing. You are still strong, affected less by disease. You get fit, both corporally and intellectually.

And then, when you turn twenty, the first symptoms of what is still in front of you begins to show.

You lose your intelligence. Your life experiences. You have less money, eventually becoming financially dependent on your parents. You go to a university and unlearn. It gets worse. Primary school and then juvenile dementia. You forget how to read and write. The state of your mind is disastrous.

When I recall the youth that is still before me, I remember the family dinners in reverse. It begins when my mother smudges plates and cutlery in a sink and then goes backward towards the table. She puts all the dirty dishes on the table and then, in various order, we sit down and uneat our meal. First, I unchew food coming out of my guts. At the end of this unchewing, a piece of pork chop comes out of my mouth. I immediately stick my fork into it and put the meat on my dirty plate. After a while, I add another piece to that chunk, and within a quarter of an hour, I have a whole, hot and fresh pork chop!

After dinner, when the plates are full, my mother takes them to the kitchen, uncooks the food, and restocks the fridge. After a few days, my mother takes it out of the fridge, puts into bags, and goes with my father to take it back to the store. They return richer than they left.

Of course, the only problem with the dinners is that afterwards you are usually hungry for a while...

Childhood is a nightmare. You shrink, you lose your mind. You spend more and more time playing silly, careless games; unbuilding block houses and demolishing sandcastles. As time passes, your words disappear. You descend into baby babble and have to wear diapers. The symptoms of infancy. This has, however, some advantages; you are not aware of the forthcoming unbirth; the end of your time in this world. It happens when you are as dumb as a bowl of pudding. You go with your mother to the hospital, and her womb absorbs you, and then she carries you around in her belly for nine months until you disappear, awareness fading with each passing day.

But right now, in my deathbirth, I am seventy-eight years old. In three years, my lovely wife, Anne, will be deathborn. My memories of her are a bit pale because of the passing of time, but I know that they will come back in a blaze of colour and sharpness at the moment of her deathbirth.

But, before her deathbirth—before her soul can step down—her body must mature inside Mother Earth. Her skeleton will be created from the dust, and then covered with guts and muscles, and with epidermis. A few days before her deathbirth, her body will be cold and pale. We'll take it out of the ground at a place called the cemetery. In a short time, her soul will penetrate into her body, and a new life begins.

***

My wife's deathbirth was the end of my repeated solitude. I felt that deep friendship and connection again; as if she was a part of me. For fifty-four years, we will have a passionate marriage, full of ecstasy and romance...and then she will disappear from my life once more. It is horrible, that I will have to lose her one day, that I will forget that she ever existed. Words can hardly describe my anguish. But, everyone has to go through this.

It is funny, how mankind regresses. Something exists, and then it doesn't. People use inventions that disappear; scientists uninvent them. We recede in an unexplained way—and it is natural. Our civilisation fades away. Computers, television sets and cars will vanish. We know nothing of what happened before our deathbirths, and with every moment, we forget what happened a while ago. We lose it irretrievably. We imagine that, as humankind, we were far more advanced than we are now; when I am young, I will be taught in school that our civilisation is on the decline. There will be two life-giving world unwars. We will end up as wild ape-men with clubs but...but it is not my problem.

Ahead of me, I have seventy-eight years of dull, predictable life, interspersed with moments of joy. I will long for them until my unbirth.

DOWN THE RABBIT HOLE

By Stacey Jaine McIntosh

The tiny glass vial I'd stolen from the witch lies drained of its sinister, illicit contents. I was only meant to take a little… Poison, even the merest sip, still has adverse side effects. My eyes shine brighter, my fingernails and lips tinge with blue, my heart galloping.

The dizzying sickness hits me hard the moment the poison enters my blood stream. It sings through my veins, warming my pale skin. I had never once considered ending my own life; but that was before I'd found myself tumbling down the rabbit hole—straight into a dark and twisted, inescapable Wonderland.

First published in *Curses and Cauldrons*, Blood Song Books, 2019

DEAR MARTHA

By Gabriella Balcom

"I stand before you with a heavy heart," Pastor Nebbens began. "With tomorrow being Valentine's Day—this is usually a happy time—but today, the death of a loved one has brought us together. Our dear sister Martha Price has departed this mortal coil. She will be greatly missed. Our thoughts and prayers go out to her husband, Thompson. May God watch over him and his family and see them through this dark time."

When the memorial service ended, people flocked to Thompson, shaking his hand, hugging him, and offering their sympathy and best wishes.

"I'm dying inside," he sobbed to an elderly lady.

"Call me anytime you want to talk," she offered.

He nodded, wiping his eyes.

But Thompson sang along with the radio on his way home. Once he arrived, he crumpled his copy of the service program, and threw it in the trash. He headed straight for his wife's jewellery box and ransacked it, tossing inexpensive pieces away and making a pile of valuables to sell.

Then he drove to the funeral home, where he'd made special arrangements to "spend more time with my sweetheart" in a private room before she was transported to the cemetery.

After locking the door behind him, he opened Martha's casket and removed her large, diamond-studded earrings. He replaced them with fakes.

Thompson frowned at her suit, wishing he'd managed to get to it before her sister, because he bet he could've returned the thing to the store. It had cost a little over $2,500, and he wanted to accumulate every penny he could. *Needed* was more accurate, since she'd cut him out of her will after catching him with another woman.

"Miserable creature," he muttered, glaring at her body. "If I'd known you'd do that, I would've poisoned you much sooner." He was tempted to slug her. She wouldn't feel it, but it would make him happy.

A glint from her hands caught his attention, though, and his eyes widened. He'd forgotten about her ring.

Thompson took Martha's left hand in his, smirking at the brilliant emerald she wore. He began sliding it off, but flinched when her finger twitched. Knowing he must've imagined that, he snorted. But he froze when it moved again.

Her hand shot toward him, squeezing his throat.

He tried to pry the appendage loose, but it tightened and pinched off his airway.

Raspy sounds filled his ears, and when he realised their source, his chest tightened. Horror made his heart gallop, but his fear and adrenaline made him stronger, and gave him just enough strength to pry the hand off.

He gulped air into his starved lungs. Unable to move, let alone run, he just tried to breathe.

Martha sat upright. Her head finally turned in his direction and her eyes popped open. They were no longer gold, but an unusual green. She parted her lips slightly but didn't speak, then grabbed Thompson and yanked him toward her.

Her mouth rapidly expanded past what was humanly possible. It became a gaping hole and enveloped his entire body.

All Thompson could manage was a faint burbling sound before her teeth pierced his body. She chewed rapidly, then gulped him down.

First published in *World of Myths Magazine*, 2020

FIRE AND ICE

By Zoey Xolton

The elemental pixie stood upon a jagged tree stump, fire and ice coursing through her veins as she surveyed the brutalised forest. Her eyes drank in the destruction, hot tears streaming down her face. She could taste the tang of iron on the air, could feel the searing pain, and hear the death cries of the felled trees.

Steeling her nerve, she followed the trail of ruin. When she found the humans responsible, she'd repay the forest's suffering three-fold! They would learn that the wilds weren't theirs to claim.

They would fear the sting of ice and bite of fire…

First published in *Hawthorn and Ash*, Iron Faerie Publishing, 2019

LOCKDOWN FANTASY #1

ABOUT THE PUBLISHER

BLACK HARE PRESS is a small, independent publisher based in Melbourne, Australia.

Founded in 2018, our aim has always been to champion emerging authors from all around the globe and offer opportunities for them to participate in speculative fiction and horror short story anthologies.

Connect

Website: *www.blackharepress.com*

Twitter: *@BlackHarePress*

LOCKDOWN FANTASY #1